Guy

Also by Jowita Bydlowska

Drunk Mom: A Memoir

Jowita Bydlowska

a novel

Guy

A BUCKRIDER BOOK

Buckrider Books is an imprint of Wolsak and Wynn Publishers.

Cover image: istockphoto.com
Cover and interior design: Michel Vrana
Author photograph: Russell Smith
Typeset in Sabon LT
Printed by Ball Media, Brantford, Canada

 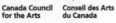 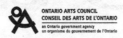 

The publisher gratefully acknowledges the support of the Canada Council for the Arts, the Ontario Arts Council and the Canada Book Fund.

Buckrider Books
280 James Street North
Hamilton, ON
Canada L8R 2L3

Library and Archives Canada Cataloguing in Publication

Bydlowska, Jowita, author
        Guy / Jowita Bydlowska.

ISBN 978-1-928088-23-3 (paperback)

        I. Title.

PS8603.Y395G89 2016   C813'.6   C2016-904661-3

To no one.

PART I

PART 1

1

THE BEACH IS FULL. IT IS ALMOST ALWAYS FULL THIS TIME
of day. There are cars parked on the sand, some with
their hatchbacks open, sudden buffets of beige and white
food – the food of the people who come to this beach. The
food of people who grow large and soft: children with apa-
thetic eyes, women with chafed thighs, men with rolls of
flesh over their hips.

There are Fours and Fives everywhere. Their eyes flick
over my face, flick away. Flick back again. I love them for
it, but the nerve. It's the media, the music videos. Every
wannabe Britney Spears thinks she is Britney Spears. But if
you were to stick the actual Britney Spears on this beach with
no handlers? After a few hours she'd be violently pink from
the sun, and her thighs would be as chafed as every other
girl's here. Unhandled, she'd be burping up yellow Cheetos.
She'd deteriorate from a Seven to a Four just like that.

A Four walks by, looks up from her phone. Small lips,
big nose. Small breasts, a belly.

"Hey," I say. I'm feeling generous. Bored. And it's a lovely evening.

"Hey?" she says.

"Great dress," I say. "It looks really good on you."

"Oh, thanks," she looks down at the dress. She blushes. It's a simple one: *on you*. As if I've seen her in other dresses. As if I were familiar. She will now hope I am familiar. Me being familiar alleviates the suspicion. Why would I be talking to her? On *you*. Her eyes big and hopeful. The dress is roomy, like a tent. It's a dress that hides things, thighs. The dress is pale green.

I don't ask for her number. I won't ask for her number. I'm suddenly tired. Not tired. I want to keep on moving. I smile and say, "Have a good night, gorgeous."

Her mouth opens, "May I pet your dog?" she says. "Please?"

"Sure," I say. I do admire nerve. She thinks she's a Seven, at least.

She bends down to pet the dog. A wave of spasm zaps through the dog's body. Pleasure. The girl's back is covered in purple stains of old acne.

"Our neighbour had a –"

Dog like this, or something. I look over to the boardwalk. The boardwalk shops are a chaos of hues. It's a landfill of flip-flops and inflatable seahorses. And plastic sunglasses and plastic pails. And dripping ice cream and the sticky fingers of children, fingers that like to reach for the dog, like the Four here.

I snap the leash, the dog's head snaps. "Have a nice day," I say.

I walk away. I don't turn around to see if she continues standing there, but I'm sure she's still standing there. I imagine soon she'll dislodge herself from our encounter, go back to her fat husband named something like Steve or Dave – Steve or Dave who will always remain confused as to why they had a horrible fight on their way back home to Dinktown, South Carolina, or wherever they're from – somewhere close by, as Steve/Dave is a nervous driver. Was it something he said?

I head toward the edge of the water. The sun is behind us, giving the ocean an orange tint. The sand is white during the day. Now it's deep yellow. Later, brown. Everything looks very nice. Everyone takes a picture with their phone. There's a grating beat of trance music in the distance.

A Two walks by. I turn to watch the back of her. You rarely see a Two, especially in a bikini: this one is a fluorescent green contraption that refuses to contain the body. Bits of her escape between the strings – an accordion of flesh. Her mouth is open, an enlarged-tonsils mouth. The one next to the Two is at least a Five. She turns around. She has a sweet face with bugging out, slanted eyes. Long, full lips. She's even odder-looking than her friend. She grins at the dog. Then it clicks for me. Of course. They must be on some kind of field trip. Short-bus field trip.

I pull the leash. The dog looks up at me. When he looks at me like that, I imagine he's winking at me. So I wink back at him. I bend down and pat his black head, sharp, black ears above a white face. A wet brown nose and blue, not brown, eyes.

My eyes, like the dog's, are blue. Women love my eyes. There are a lot of other things about my face that women love, I've been told. I have good cheekbones. My mouth with its corners curling up a bit, a wide smile.

Then there's the rest of me. A strong, well-defined body. Lean and muscular. You might think: athlete. No tattoos, no scars except for a pale line on my shin from a bike accident. Tall enough, the third-tallest boy in class. Caucasian. Dark hair. Slightly tanned. A nice dick, seven-plus inches, cut. Shoe size, eleven; chest, forty-two regular; waist, thirty-four – an eight-inch drop. The neck, sixteen-point-five. Perfect proportions. But we're not shopping for clothes here, so all of this simply means *I look good*.

Presently, I get to the end of the sandy patch where there's a small shack, a beach eatery. It serves "healthy smoothies." This is a euphemism for thick, mud-green liquid. Brutalized fruit and veggies. Protein powder. A sticky, sugary taste in your mouth.

I'm not here for the smoothies. The real reason I'm here is because the smoothies are the perfect girl snack. The place is swarming with girls. Sunburned, giggly girls that come from the beige inns. Or from the cheaply built beach houses. Or they come out of the hatchbacks of their parents' cars. Giggly, jiggly girls determined to atone for last night's beer and pizza with sugary mud. Girls keen on shedding their parents' white-food values. Girls promising their growing belly bulges that they will eat better from now on: smoothies, water, grass.

There are a few tables outside the shack and a couple of smaller tables inside where there are computers. Girls in their cheapo beachwear squirm around screens watching videos of the latest pop sensation, whoever it is – lately, $isi. The smoothie cups sit empty, abandoned on the window ledges.

Today, there's the usual throng of girls gathered around the computer screens. $isi's latest hit, "Brokenhearted," bounces off the walls. There's a coconut smell of tanning oil in the air. The girls sweat and vibrate with excitement. The song has a cocaine line of a hook. I remember a producer saying that a song is a success if you can't imagine you could ever stop listening to it. But then you run out of your high, and only $isi can give you the right fix again.

And only people like me can give you $isi.

I have a sudden image of $isi tiptoeing to a bathroom. We're in a hotel. A dark room, a vast white bed, me in it. She is holding herself between her legs. There's sunlight cutting through the slit in the curtains. It divides the carpet in a straight, bright line, $isi's brown feet turning white as she steps through it. She says, "I always thought that was a cliché, sleeping with people to get ahead in life."

"You feel used?"

She turns toward me, "Not at all. Make me a star."

I can't see her after staring at her feet, at the bright line for too long. Everything – her face – has vanished. Then it all comes back slowly, the contours of her face. Small and narrow, a mouse face. The clamped mouth. She looks like a child pretending not to be a child. But she is no longer a child. I'm not her downfall; I am her saviour. I will make her into a star.

I do make her into a star.

* * *

I line up behind a Seven and a maybe-Four and a solid Three.

There's some problem with the smoothie machine. Panicked bustling behind the counter.

"She was so sad when I saw her in that video," says the Three.

"How do you know she was sad? Oh my god, it's all just for show," says maybe-Four. She's got a look that's all wrong. Her hair is wild and curly. There's a lot of it, uncombed. Glasses, too. She's either a lesbian-in-training or this is a pretty-girl-trying-to-be-ugly thing. Some men consider that cute. I don't. I consider it tiresome.

The Seven says, "I read on Perez that she, like, had a big breakup, but she won't talk about it because she's, like, becoming media-smart, so she's just giving hints and stuff to the press."

"Please," the maybe-Four says.

"I don't know, I just read it online."

"Yeah, when I saw her in the video, she really seemed totally genuine," says the Three. In the same moment she looks up and sees me. She blinks. Looks down.

The maybe-Four says, "Dolly, look at me, look, look. Guess if I'm sad or not, come on, look." She relaxes her forehead, her dark eyes suddenly turning softer, bigger, bushy eyebrows going up a little above the glasses.

The Three shakes her head, "Very mature." She looks behind the Seven. Looks at me again. She does this quickly, nervously. It's like a tick, that quick glance.

I take in her face. It's perfect. It's round and a little flat with zero cheekbones. The chin is round, but already propped up by a promise of a second fold. She's not fat. She's well nourished. For now. Her eyes are the best feature. Round, doll-like eyes with supremely white whites, sugar whites, baby eyes.

It's almost always in the eyes. The hope and belief and freshness that nothing can recreate as a girl gets older. Sometimes you see it in celebrities, the baby-bright eyes. But that's all artificial, mechanics at work. Armies of professionals and products: the liquids and lights that hide the yellowness of spray tan, the paleness of heroin, tiredness and heartbreak.

"This is so annoying," the maybe-Four says to no one in particular. She says it loudly enough to get one of the women behind the counter to look up in our direction. The woman's eyebrows knot and unknot.

"Em, be quiet," the Seven hisses.

The Three looks at me again. This time I invite her eyes into mine. I don't look away. I don't smile yet either. I just let the eyes do the talking – mine pulling and hers coming forward. Closer and closer until it's pupil to pupil, my eyes engulfing hers in the sort of promise that she's just started to look for in life. *Open wide. My engorged dick in your mouth*, I say with my eyes.

I can sense the internal squirm: she wants to blink. But she doesn't blink.

Let me fuck you. Let me show you, teach you. Let me free you from your dumb, sad life for at least a few moments. Turn you over on all fours. Tell you I love your breasts, your ass. Pull your hair a little, make you gasp.

Her head twitches, eyes down.

There's more noise behind the counter, near the smoothie machine. Someone shouts that it's working. The girls in front of me stop talking. The line moves forward and they move with it.

The Three looks one more time, and now I smile: *Put your hand right here. See how hard you're making me?*

* * *

Outside the shack, the dog is panting in the sun. An aggressively serious woman with yoga gear enveloping her flat, athletic body walks by and stops abruptly. Her face softens when the dog jumps with a stifled bark as I come out with my smoothie. A former Six, now a Four; she's slowly turning into a thoroughbred horse; you can see her youth falling off her.

I go up to the dog to make a show of petting him. I tell him he's a good dog.

I praise my dog for things like sitting and shitting and eating. If he could sing, I could make him a pop star. Same IQs.

I check out my Facebook page to see if anyone's commented on the rockfish with tomato sauté and brown rice. No one. When I look up, the woman is walking away. Her ass is nice, but she probably hates its plumpness that refuses to be processed by the gym equipment.

The three girls come out and start to push patio chairs around one of the tables. They're talking in whispers. I can feel the excitement. Without looking, I know they're looking at us, my dog and me.

I check my Facebook again. Homemade ravioli, one comment: "nice!" Someone named Cassandra. I have a vague memory of armpit stubble scraping my nose.

There's a scrunch of sand and clacking of flip-flops behind me. "What's your dog's name?"

I turn around. It's the Seven. Her face is a triangle of well-arranged cheekbones. Pointy chin, full lips. There's hardness in her eyes that only comes from knowing that you're pretty.

"Dog. The dog's name is Dog," I say and her hard, clear eyes widen for a second and then squint.

She says in a flat voice, "That's funny."

"It's *very* funny."

"Actually, my friend wants to know. She's obsessed with dogs," she says.

"Well, it's Dog. It's easy to remember."

"Dolores, come over here," she shouts.

Dolores, the sweet, well-nourished Three, blushes a big blush that comes right through her sunburned cheeks. She gets up from the table.

Who names a girl *Dolores*? It's mean, like naming her *Gladys* or *Bertie*. It's like naming a girl after her grandmother who was courageous because she survived the Nazis. Or had many children on the prairie somewhere and once amputated her own leg in the dead of winter, while running. But *Dolores* it is, and it's perfect. It's perfect that she's stuck with the name of an old lady, more humiliating somehow.

I watch Dolores walk. She's got the barely-lifting-her-feet walk. In her flip-flops, she shuffles. It's the walk of weekends in pajamas, evenings in front of the TV – a bowl of Lucky Charms and a glass of warm milk – the walk of slouching from class to class, panting runs around the gymnasium and moving side to side if forced to dance at the school prom, where she went with her gay best friend. It's the walk of a girl who doesn't want to be noticed, and I notice every single thing about it.

"Hi," she says, to me or to the dog. She sits down on the wet sand, facing the dog and stroking his stupid, happy face.

"Hi. He likes you," I tell her, and she looks up. Our eyes do their thing – mine telling hers that I like her. Hers unsure, but already rushing in, getting swallowed.

"Dolores used to have a dog but it got hit by a car, right?" the Seven says.

Dolores blinks and nods solemnly and says, "His name was Punky. It was my dad's dog. An Akita."

I'm impressed. I know enough about dogs to know that an Akita is not an easy dog. It's a large animal. Bigger than mine, with muscular though slim shoulders and paws twice the size of Dog's. It's a dog of single guys or couples – never couples with children. I wonder if Dolores' parents are divorced. *My dad's dog* clearly suggests that.

"I'm sorry to hear that."

The Seven says, "Dolores was pretty bummed out, right?"

"It's okay," Dolores says. "This is Kelly," meaning the Seven, who looks a little startled by suddenly being introduced. She thrusts a little pink-nailed paw at me.

I say, "Hi, Kelly. I'm Guy, nice to meet you."

"Guy's your name?"

"Yes."

Ready? One, two, three!

"That's funny. So you have a dog named Dog, and you're a guy named Guy?" Kelly says.

"That *is* funny," I say. "And you're Dolores?" I say to Dolores, who nods. She has broken eye contact to look into the eyes of the dog named Dog.

"Dog. Nice to meet you," she says to the dog, who says nothing.

The maybe-Four remains at the table throughout this exchange. She's absorbed in her phone, slurping her smoothie, but now she looks up. She wrinkles her forehead. I consider smiling. But no. I can tell she's the kind of girl who'll call me a perv to her friends the moment I leave: "Did you see the way that perv was smiling at me? Fucking gross."

It's time to go anyway. I'm sure I got this. Just look at Dolores trying not to look at me.

Kelly moves her hand to shield her face from the sun, "So you live around here?" She's trying on confidence.

"Vacation. The grey house over there," I point in the direction of the beach house. It's a four-bedroom, two-garage nautical castle complete with solar panels and white wooden columns that support all three decks. It belongs to me, paid for courtesy of my grandmother's will.

"The big grey one? Dope," Kelly says.

"House-sitting for my friend," I say. *Dope.*

"Not yours?" she says, her voice like a sigh. I imagine her life already taking shape: assessing and comparing friends' possessions. One friend's car, another friend's pool. Another friend's graduation party. Just like her mother, probably, with her friends' Botox jobs, husbands, summer homes and children graduating from prestigious colleges. "Nice gig," she says.

"It is. Well, it was nice to meet you. Gotta take this guy home."

"Which guy?" says the maybe-Four from the picnic table. How could she hear that far?

"Nice to meet you too," says Dolores. "Nice to meet you, Dog."

I walk away. The sky is turning even bloodier around the edges. The beach is famous for its spectacular sunsets. Around this time, you start seeing the beach people holding their phones up, taking pictures of the sun. Romantics.

I know that Dolores is looking at me walking away. She sees my wide back, the way my calves spasm slightly. A twitch that lasts a moment too long. I've had women tell me that I strut a little. This used to bother me, but it doesn't anymore. It's not a put-on strut like what my best friend, Jason, does with his walk. He's just trying hard to not be mediocre, which he is.

For me, the way I move, it's natural.

"It's like you're trying to pick a fight," Gloria, my girl-friend, said once.

But I'm not trying to pick a fight.

Just the opposite.

2

AS A CHILD, I LIVED WITH MY MOTHER, MY SISTER AND MY father in a small town in Ontario, Canada, where everyone knew that the dentist was a drunk and that the one, part-time homeless lady lost her kid in a freak accident in a silo after her husband had left her for the drunken dentist's receptionist. There was a library and a courthouse in our small town. Also, three high schools. My mother taught at one of the high schools. My father worked at the courthouse.

My early childhood was uneventful. There was one funeral – my mother's mother, whose will divided the family, with us ending up on the lucky side – and one birth – my younger sister.

At twelve, I was a well-adjusted boy. No setting things on fire or drinking my mother's vodka. I never did drugs. I was not into upsetting my parents since that would draw their attention to me. This is why I never bothered telling my father about walking in on my mother touching hands with our neighbour, Karl. Karl who – I could always sense – wanted to, or had done so and wanted to again, fuck my mother. It was doglike, the way they seemed to pant at each other as they talked.

I also never got caught with my pants rolled down in my mother's underwear drawer, spending myself right into the wooden corners of it. That was probably the most troubling sexual thing that I'd done in my life. I've never done truly creepy things like touch my little sister when tasked with changing her shitty diaper. (The takeaway? It's not my fault she was anorexic in her twenties.)

Overall, I was a good kid. So it was a surprise to everyone when Caroline happened. The way I think of it – *Caroline happened* – is intentional. It was an event, like a hurricane, threatening enough that it gets its own name. Though looking back on it, it was more like Guy happened to Caroline; perhaps that's what she would say.

Caroline was one of my mother's students. My mother had an altruistic side, and she provided tutoring for the underprivileged kids.

Every Tuesday and Thursday evening, the basement filled with those retards sitting or standing beside my mother at a large table, their homework spread out in front of them like war maps.

Caroline was older than me, fifteen to my thirteen. But she looked closer to my age with her almost breastless body. She was not pretty. Not only that, she wasn't even ugly. She was just something drawn randomly. A bunch of squiggles and lines that made up the form of a girl so incredibly uninteresting that she immediately fascinated me. I could not understand it fully, or explain it to myself as I acknowledged it. It was as if her lack of attractiveness was some kind of a vacuum for my attractiveness. We complemented each other that way.

The first time I saw her, she was holding some papers in her hand, nervously. She wanted to read her homework to my mother or something. Something that stressed her out. I stressed her out too. Before I turned away, I sensed her attention on me. You can tell those things. I remember the intensity, the urging...the desperation even, as I felt it. Was she in trouble, and was I the only person capable of saving her? Her attention was thrilling, the obviousness of it, the way it surrounded me and made me feel powerful, big. A big boy.

"You're so adorable," she said later, in a mocking way. "You're like my annoying little brother."

She was probably unaware of the fact that the whole time she was scanning me, I was thinking about things I had seen in German nudie mags. What would it look like to shove my dick in her mouth? Or flip her onto all fours to try to penetrate her? I was imagining pinching her tiny nipples till she squeaked. I knew about the things people did to each other. I was always good at research.

* * *

She started staying longer after her tutoring lessons, and my parents didn't mind. We sat in the backyard – it was spring – and talked. I dwelled on the details of her. A tiny braided bracelet. How delicate it looked wrapped around the protruding wrist bone. I wanted to take the bracelet in my mouth, taste the dirty threads that had accumulated her sweat.

Her knees. A dark spot from a scab that left a mark, like a kitten's paw. Also, the way her hair looked wet on a hot day when it got too greasy from being outside. Or how she scratched the side of her leg and then would sometimes clean the same nail with her bottom teeth, which was disgusting, but somehow wasn't.

She was a collection of images, impressions – artifacts that I'd bag up and file for later. All those images, parts of Caroline brought out something in me – a need to be in contact with another human being. Not just any human being: her, specifically. It was sexual, but it was not exactly about sex. I couldn't tell what it was. It felt as if there was a short-circuit in my brain, some pleasant malfunction. Yet. I was troubled by this need; it was as if I absolutely had to be around her all the time. It was like the flu. I hoped it would pass. I wasn't sure if this was okay, what I felt. In retrospect, it was probably just puberty.

* * *

Sometime near the end of the summer, I lost my virginity to Caroline. It happened on the weekend when my parents were away with my younger sister.

Caroline undressed me like I was a child. She undressed herself.

We lay side by side on my parents' bed. We stared at each other. Looked over each other's bodies. Our bodies were foreign planets, newly discovered.

We didn't talk.

I had already guessed the outlines of her breasts and predicted the flat stomach. But I was still shocked by her neat-but-bushy mound. It was the same mousy colour as the hair on her head. It seemed very exotic. She looked nothing like the hairless women from the nudie magazines full of pneumatic lips and tits.

She pulled me on top of her and aimed my dick at her little vagina. She moved her hips. I figured I had to move along with her, and as I did I penetrated her. She was soft and wet inside. Hot like breath. It was like nothing I'd ever experienced before. It was eternally comforting. I was falling into her softness. Too fast, too recklessly.

I came.

She laughed with delight and then wrapped her arms around me, hugging me; she was bigger than me. After we fell apart, she snuggled up to me. She breathed "I love you" into my neck.

Immediately, I started to develop a headache. It was the sort of headache you get from running for too long or some other strenuous physical effort. I was in no way exhausted from the sex. Yet the headache was creeping in regardless. Something else was happening, too.

I felt it first physically. It started with her arm. Her arm around me got heavy, as if it was her leg instead. Her body next to me became too long. There seemed to be no escape from it.

Still, her heat and smell made my own body respond with an intensity that terrified me. I gripped my dick. I held it, feeling it get hard. I wondered if by sleeping with Caroline I had unleashed something bad. Was I now capable of violence? Murder? I felt capable of it. I didn't know where it came from. I didn't know what to do but to lie still until it passed. I kept thinking of fucking: her, the women in nudie mags. My mother too, or someone who was like my mother. My homeroom teacher.

I wanted to run. I wanted to push my dick right back into Caroline. Her heavy arm kept me pinned to the mattress. I imagined that the arm pinning me down was capable of protecting me from whatever was happening inside me. I kept still. I waited. I let go of my dick.

Eventually, I fell asleep and dreamt of being covered in thick, dense blankets.

* * *

After that weekend, things were different between Caroline and me. I developed other acquaintances in the neighbourhood: boys. I spent my afternoons playing video games in their basements, or smoking in the garbage-infested park by the river that ran through town.

One evening, Caroline accosted me on my way home. The meadow near our house was loud with buzzing insects. She came out of the darkness and threw herself at me.

I did nothing. I let her hold me with my arms at my sides like a doll. I imagined myself to be a doll. Like a doll, I waited patiently for it to be over, to be put back in my box. Instead, Caroline tried to kiss me.

I moved my face away until she stopped trying to kiss me. She needed to leave me alone. I said that. I thought she would understand – it would free her up too, to have more time to spend with friends.

"You little piece of shit."

I felt my dick stir. It confused me. "I'm sorry," I said.

I noticed then that she had changed her look. She was wearing makeup. Her hair was blonder. She dyed it, like my mom. She was trying to make herself pretty. If I had been a little piece of shit, I would've said something to her about it – how it didn't work – but I wasn't even sure that it didn't work. Maybe she was prettier now?

"Do you love me?" Her voice sounded small and angry, like an ugly little animal that peeped after being stepped on.

"No. I don't think so," I said, truthfully.

"I hate you."

"Okay."

"Okay?" She pushed me away. She lifted her hand as if to slap me. She stroked my cheek instead. And then, for a brief moment, I felt what I had felt before, the longing.

"I'm sorry," I said. I didn't mean it. But her face softened.

"You don't even know," she said.

She said other things after that. Things I've heard again many times. Not from her, but from others: that I had opened up something in her, that she had changed because of me, that I made her feel beautiful.

How?

I didn't know.

"I'll be okay," she said, finally, and I thought what happened was a good thing, that I had done a good thing. I knew then I would do it again. I'd get better at it. I knew that I was capable of changing someone, someone plain and insignificant like Caroline, of turning her into a person who could light up from inside, if even for a moment.

It was like magic. I wanted to make that magic again (and again!) because that was what I seemed to be good at. I wanted another Caroline, another devotion like that. I believe I became instantly addicted to it. You cannot fight addiction. It installs itself in your head and doesn't leave. You can try to control it. But it's always there, a faint whisper somewhere behind you.

***

Caroline ended up dating a senior from her high school. He didn't knock her up. She didn't drop out of school to do drugs. She didn't become obese. She finished school and went to college to become a nurse. She became a nurse and eventually renewed friendship with my mother when my mother was dying of cancer in the hospital where Caroline worked. I felt proud of how well Caroline turned out.

3

AFTER CAROLINE, DESPITE MY NEWLY DISCOVERED PASSION, the post-sex repulsion happened almost every time. I'd sleep with a girl and then I'd want her gone. Instinctively, I'd pick the girls who were used to having to go. I suppose it was exactly like addiction: excitement, remorse. Confusion. Compulsion.

The girls I fucked asked no questions. They carried condoms in their purses. They always seemed happy if I asked them to stay the night, but they were also prepared to pick their clothes off the floor in the dark and let themselves out before dawn.

In college, these were the girls who published articles about how much they loved themselves and their curves, but they'd show an absolute disregard for themselves if I suggested a blow job in the back of the car. The next week they would march around campus with signs, screaming about men raping them with their eyes, about wanting to go topless and so on.

I ignored the hysteria. It didn't exist. It had nothing to do with me. I was not going to politicize my sex life. Sexually, I had my own interests. My neuroses were my biggest concern. I carried on my usual internal battle: one hour I'd be obsessing over some ridiculous trait like the way a girl hooked her ankle around the other ankle; the way she would defend it, later, that gymnastic feat, like she didn't mean it. She meant it. They meant it. It was meant to impress me.

* * *

There were so many girls, and many didn't even leave more than a wisp of memory. Their artifacts: two moles beside each other on a face; a fat back; cellulite-ribbed thighs; stretch marks on flat breasts; inverted nipples; a hairy stomach; a row of small, even teeth; teeth with too much gums; red, round knees like heads; very long labia minora; etcetera. They had their smells: mint, burnt sugar, cigarettes and candy, vanilla, cookies, old books, cinnamon, Korean noodle shop, alcohol, perfume that brought tears to my eyes, shit, spit, urine, formaldehyde.

Yet, I was never able to maintain interest for more than a few dates.

"Should I call you a cab?"

She, they, always said *no*. And then she, they, would go.

* * *

But, eventually, spending so much time on a campus infested with feminist hysteria did have its effect. I became convinced it was my duty to feel bad about these encounters. Or at least to act as if I felt bad.

I gave up sex for a while, but women were always around me, always flashing their smiles and widening their eyes. There were so many women, so many signals that needed responding to. How could I ignore it? I did, though. I felt holy, like a priest. I lived a pure life.

I stopped going out. I locked myself in my dorm room. I paced and paced. I lay on my bed and thought of a song I heard once in a sad girl's dorm room. I fucked this girl after a poetry book launch. She was the poet. She had a small face, rat teeth, a purple cloud of hair. In her room, we sat on the floor. A skinny dog named after a flower tried to nip at my ankles and she locked it in the bathroom. She drank vodka and smoked. She said she knew I would fuck her and never call her again. She played the song that went like this: "Is that all there is?"

That was the line that kept playing in my head: *Is that all there is?* I felt embarrassed about having it play in my head, but at least I wasn't doing it in front of another person like the poet girl. Also, I thought it was a good sign that I still cared about things like that – about embarrassing myself.

Eventually, because of my confusion, I began to think I was going crazy. The campus posters suggested seeing therapists. I went to see one. She said I was stressed, possibly needed a break. I was okay – academically – but I felt unsafe. I listened to the suggestion. I reported myself as if I was a person reporting another person.

I went to a hospital. It didn't seem like a terrible idea. I enjoy new experiences.

I spent two days talking to mental-health professionals, reading magazines and eating Jell-O. I told one of the psychiatrists about feeling embarrassed about a song playing in my head, but also how I thought that was a good sign.

"What kind of song?"

"An old classic. A song from my childhood that my mother used to play. I miss my childhood," I said.

"Why is it a good sign? To hear this song?"

"I think it shows that I'm invested," I said, and the psychiatrist nodded. She had straight black hair, dyed, harsh. I imagined holding it in fistfuls, pulling it like reins.

I left that session and slid around the hallway in my slippers. It was the first time I wore slippers round the clock since childhood. As predicted, there was a certain sense of adventure to it all.

I was not crazy, and I didn't want to die. If I'd wanted to die, I'd have known it. It was time to re-evaluate. I had no religion, but there were things I believed in. Like my nature. I talked to psychiatrists about that. How I wanted to re-evaluate, how I wanted to live in accordance to my nature.

"What is your nature?"

"I like people. Ultimately, I like people. I want to find a girlfriend."

"This doesn't sound too bad to me."

"I don't know."

"Are you hurting anyone? Your guilt is only hurting you."

"You're right. That is very perceptive."

It *was* perceptive. I hoped it showed in my face that I was getting better already. It did show. The psychiatrist was pleased, I could tell. She leaned back in her chair. I thought how the pink blouse was a great colour on her, how it offset her brown skin. I wanted to lick her, taste her skin. It was impossible to tell what kind of tits she had. I was sure she was wearing one of those shield bras, round and padded.

"I look forward to finishing school," I said.

The psychiatrist smiled. I was saying all the right things.

I left the hospital without the burden of guilt. I would say I even felt optimistic about life.

4

AROUND THAT TIME, MY FRIEND JASON JOINED A PICKUP
artist group, where men talked about strategies for hitting
on women. This movement was probably a kind of reaction to the rabid man-hate that was everywhere. The men
exchanged tips and stories on message boards. Occasionally,
the PUAs – as Jason called them – would meet in real life.
He took me to their meet-up one night. There were twenty
men in a basement, most of them young like me and Jason.

A paunchy man got up and talked nonsense. He wore a
T-shirt that read *Tool*. He had black spacers in his ears. The
name of the band combined with his overall dweebiness and
the circumstances he was in did not escape my sense of irony.

Tool said he went *sarging for HBs*. He approached *a
warm-up set of two*. He *locked in,* but then he got *locked out*
by a third HB before he managed to give his number to a *set*.

Jason whispered "hot babe" when the HB term came
up again. Other than that, I was on my own. My phone
vibrated. It was a text from some girl that she must've sent

drunk. Something about me being a dick. The PUA chief kept prattling on about his various failures with women. He recited acronyms with a forced casualness.

I looked around at all the other pasty basement-dwellers who would one day crawl out like the sad, wormy things they were and – armed with tips from message boards from other dweebs – crawl to their shopping malls. There, they would spread their slime around until some sad victim got stuck in it long enough for them to recite their lines. The humiliations they put themselves through – attacking women in shopping malls, bragging about their attacks, whining about being shot down, their language full of hurt and vitriol. It was horrifyingly stupid. Absurd. Unsophisticated.

I was not absurd or unsophisticated.

After Tool, another tool got up to speak. He was attractive, blond like a Viking. Why was *he* here? My guess was it had something to do with the size of his penis. The Viking looked around the room and smiled: "Men, remember, women want to be seduced, and a well-done pickup is a gift to women."

"He is *sooo* good," Jason said in a squeaky whisper.

The Viking told an anecdote about sleeping with a woman and telling her he had to leave to make it back to the bar before last call. All the men laughed. I didn't get a chance to find out if this was a cautionary tale or a practice that was advocated because I got up and left. Jason told me later that during the break, the men joked that I was probably a fag or a feminist.

The truth was, despite its ridiculousness, that meeting reminded me how thrilling the pursuit of women actually was. I didn't need a workshop. I didn't want motivational speeches telling me how to seduce a woman. I didn't have to read books about it, listen to tips about how it was best to fire in *all* directions because it was statistically guaranteed that I'd eventually hit something. I've always hit the bull's eye anyway.

I decided to start *dating*. This time, I wanted to date beautiful girls. I don't mean dogs in clingy dresses, with plucked eyebrows, Marilyn Monroe delusions, fake lashes and duck pouts.

Only dweeby PUAs would fall for that.

By *beautiful*, I mean actresses, models and club girls. I knew the methods of picking up beautiful girls were barely more sophisticated than methods of picking up one-nighter girls. The truth was most girls liked you to be direct, and most girls liked to be degraded. There's a subtlety to it all that escapes amateurs like my friend Jason, who only offends girls by saying things like, "I like your moustache" to tease them, or by coming on too aggressively, saying, "We should go to my place and fuck."

***

Around this time, I got a job through my father's friend who ran a magazine for men. I set up photo shoots and wrote small articles about products: razors, nail clippers. Occasionally, I got to test a sports car and write about it, but mostly it was photo shoots and men's clothing. There were lots of parties: launches of products, festivals, charity events. The women at these events were Eights and Nines, with long hair and long legs, bouncy tits and firm asses.

It was too much at once. It was time to settle on something. Someone. I couldn't keep fantasizing. I'd atrophy my confidence and end up in some PUA basement.

One evening, I said to a Nine, "You're nothing like those model types."

She was definitely a model. Pouty. Honey-blond hair, big eyes. "What do you mean?"

"I mean, you are. But there's something else about you. You look...too real to be a model."

She widened those big eyes. The large forehead wrinkled and stayed that way.

I knew enough about beautiful girls to know that their beauty destroyed them. They would fall apart at the smallest thing. I knew that my girl would see *real* as *imperfect*, perhaps even *fat*. I knew that from then on, she would think I held the answers to what she was. A model? A real person? Fat? Imperfect? I was subtler than Jason. I only served doubt, a delicate weapon like a long needle.

We dated for a month. Sandra. It was exhausting. I quickly realized that with beauty came demands and neediness so disproportionate to what I had to offer that my feeling of dread had me in its thrall almost the entire time.

"It's not you, it's me."

"You can't even try to come up with something more original, can you?" she said.

I could, but why bother my brain?

I went on dates with more beautiful girls, and it was always the same thing as it was with Sandra. The demands remained baroque, just like their beauty. Demands for more time, more attention, more everything, more me. I had no *me* to give. I've always hated sharing.

I reflected on how beauty affected girls. Beautiful women live beautiful clichés: models and moguls. Favouritism in the family, the pretty sister always somehow better than the plain one. Free drinks, free dinners, weekends in chalets. Free trips to Europe and free cocaine, free everything.

Beauty can be a ticket to a better life. Beautiful women expect more. It's no surprise that they become indignant if *more* takes its time, become bitter if *more* isn't happening, become tragic if it happens and disappears. Because once they understand their advantage, there is no turning back. There is no extracting Cinderella from her Louboutins and stuffing her back into clogs. As soon as they catch a whiff of their advantage, beautiful girls become obsessed with getting their ticket to a better life punched as soon as possible. And as a boyfriend, I was not punching the ticket. I dumped them. I left them open-mouthed in disbelief that I even dared. In the beginning, occasionally, it seemed the joke was on me and I would get confused, thinking it was stupid to let the Good Thing go.

But then I would remember the one rule of beauty: its simple presence made you feel as if you were receiving something special. Beauty's greatest deceit – the same one I take advantage of – is that you shouldn't disregard it. It is exactly how I use my own gift with women.

* * *

It was a relief, an expansion of space, when I went back to what felt most natural – being with girls to whom I was

God's gift. I had a rabid taste for plain girls. It came from the imprint of my first sexual experience. And, naturally, plain girls are easier to handle. Although there was some effort required, I was not resentful of it: I enjoyed seducing plain girls. They adored me. I remembered the power that I had with Caroline. I had to prove nothing to her to be everything to her. It was so easy to let go of her.

I decided to turn the seduction of plain girls into a lifetime pursuit. At that time, it wasn't a conscious decision, but it became one later, once it was clear what gave me the most satisfaction.

My life opened to grateful girls. Girls with weight problems and with bad skin. Girls who had dreams, but who could forsake those dreams because they understood from the time they were born that the world would not give into their demands. The world was unapologetic about loving beauty, and it ignored the plain girls, if not downright rebuked them.

I had the power to be the world to them.

* * *

Unlike Sandra, I don't remember the name of the first plain girl I dated, but I do remember her gratitude and her lack of expectation. Even dumping her seemed easier. There was some resignation, some offhand comment, but that was that and it was done with. Months later, she sent me a nice letter saying that I was really special, that I had created one of her most treasured memories.

Katie. Cathy?

I suppose I should remember her name, but it didn't really matter. She might as well have written on behalf of all the girls who followed and who declared me some kind of deity that – even temporarily – relieved them of their insignificance.

Then it was just a matter of time: getting used to their sloppiness and neediness, learning how to navigate properly so as not to set their hopes too high yet leave enough lovely memories and magic in their lives to make them forever indebted to me. It was back to, "So you want me to leave?"

"Do you mind letting the dog back in when you do?"

"Sure. Here's my number just in case."

* * *

I didn't have to feel badly about them, or even act as if I felt badly. They were always grateful. And knowing this made sex with them more meaningful. What happened in the beginning, with Caroline, and with all the easy women after her, was gone. There was no dread, no self-torture about how to keep it going, how to maintain the façade. I no longer lied to myself that this should mean more than it meant. No one would hold me accountable for not sticking around. The plain girls simply didn't expect it. I pleased them. The end.

5

I WATCH THE BEACH FROM THE LIFEGUARD CHAIR I HAD installed in front of my beach house. I watch to see if I can find Dolores among the beach people. Even if she were there, I wouldn't be able to tell her apart from all the others. All the sweet, chubby girls with round shoulders and bad dye jobs.

I picture her walking slowly, her feet splayed, sleep still clouding her lovely eyes, her cheeks getting red from the effort. Thighs rubbing against each other. There are many Doloreses on the beach today.

Later on, at the beach house, as I set the table, I see the actual Dolores. It's her and the other two girls walking by, looking in. I back away from the window even though there's no way they can see me with the light reflecting off the glass. Dolores' mouth is slightly open. Eyes scanning the window.

I could go out, say hello, but the guests will be arriving any minute. I don't want the girls, Dolores especially, to get the wrong impression. And she'd get the wrong impression seeing Gloria and her magnificent figure, the way she seems to be cut out of one of those luxury magazines about yachts. There's little chance Gloria will be affectionate – she's not the type – but you never know with Jason, who may say something about us, about me and Gloria being *lovebirds* or something like that.

The girls pass eventually, and I go back to making lunch: a salad with goat cheese, red pepper strips, spicy glazed pecans, apple slices on a bed of mixed field greens. Rye-bread toast.

My phone rings. It's probably Jason, dying to report the sort of sights you see as you enter the beach town: the rickety roller coaster and merry-go-round, the minigolf and the go-karts, all of it damaged, in need of a new paint job. Jason is a city boy, and the local folklore would excite him.

But it's not Jason. It's $isi. She sounds sleepy. Her voice is childlike, but already getting raw from the bad things she enjoys too much. "Guy. There was a situation."

"With the video?"

"No. Not with the video."

"With what then, sweetheart?"

"You'll see. I'm sorry," she says. "Some asshole took a photo–"

"What kind of photo?"

"Oh, you know."

"No, I don't know. Are your tits showing in the photo? Because if your tits are showing in the photo, that's not really a bad thing."

Silence.

"$isi."

"Don't say *tits*, please," she says. "It wasn't anything like that. But like I said, it's not good."

"You didn't actually say that."

"I'm saying it now."

I want to hang up on her. I want to call Mark, her manager, and find out what kind of photo we're talking about. But before I do that, I also want to get her reaction to the numbers on YouTube. It would be a good thing to hear her acknowledge the numbers. The biggest problem with $isi is that she's not motivated enough lately.

"Did you see the numbers?" I ask. I hate it that she won't say it first because asking her makes me look like I'm begging, like I'm begging for some kind of approval.

"Yeah. We killed."

"Yeah. Good girl."

"Don't say that. Don't call me that. That's what you call me when you fuck me."

"I don't fuck you," I say, and she slams the phone.

I call Mark. The photo turns out to be of $isi smoking a joint. As far as drugs go, this isn't the worst, nothing like Amy Winehouse and her crack pipe, but fuck.

"She's been dealing with a lot of things lately," Mark says. His voice is wavering. I wonder if Mark is still mad about me being one of those things. I want to remind him that, thanks to me, $isi will probably become the biggest up-and-coming star of some month in the future – or if we're lucky, a whole season. The new Britney. Now might be the perfect time to talk about a Thing we need for $isi – a signature scandal. Like a sex tape, or kissing Tila Tequila, or nipple tassels shooting confetti. A joint is not it.

"No, a joint is not it," Mark sighs.

"Her estranged mother?"

"God."

"Something else then. A stalker? A feud. With Rihanna?"

"Nobody fights with Rihanna. She's too cool."

"A shotgun wedding."

"We don't have anyone lined up," Mark says.

"Let's call Piglet."

"Who?"

"Jennifer," I say.

Jennifer lives in Los Angeles. She is one of $isi's publicists who specializes in making up believable shit for the media whenever one of her many clients flashes her drunken pussy or holds a funny-looking vial, or a funny-looking cigarette, or falls into cactuses outside of Le Chateau Shitface. She also comes up with Things, and she's a clean-scandal pro, more Almost-See-Through Dress than Sucking Off Famous Athlete.

I have never met Jennifer in person. We kept missing each other. The only reason I don't freak out over never having met her is because she's supposed to be the best. But I hate not knowing what she looks like – me not knowing what she looks like gives her an advantage.

I google images of "Jennifer Jones Evan Public Relations." The only image that Google comes up with is the same picture of a laughing piglet that she keeps on the website bio.

"Why *Piglet*? Never mind. Oh, yeah, did you end up getting tested?" Mark says.

My body goes numb. For a second, I even feel like crying. I don't know what's worse, feeling like crying or Mark knowing, but then I picture Dr. Babe, which is not her actual name but what Jason called her once and it stuck.

I got tested only a month ago. Dr. Babe peeled the top plastic off of the swab package. She was wearing a long skirt, a lavender blouse that billowed around her thin arms; her hair was straightened. No eye makeup. In my mind, I lifted her up and spread her legs, feet in the stirrups. I hiked up her skirt. I ripped a side of her panties with forceps. I stuffed the panties in her mouth. I kneeled and buried my nose in her dark little cunt. Her moans were muffled by the panties; she clutched my hair with her tiny hands. *Good girl*, I said, and she writhed. They love it when I call them that: *Good girl*.

The swab pinched inside the tip of my dick; it hurt as if a needle shot through my entire body, exploding in my brain before disappearing, along with my fantasy of Dr. Babe in the stirrups.

"Almost done," Dr. Babe said sweetly.

After I got dressed, we talked about where she was going to go on vacation. To the UK for her sister's wedding. I imagined her sister in this office, watching us: Dr. Babe's legs in stirrups as I ate her out.

The tests came back negative; I didn't have a single STI. I don't know why I panicked about that tiny rash, and I have no idea why I told Mark about it.

"I'm okay. At least you never have to worry about that stuff," I say to Mark, who is perpetually single.

"Very funny."

"Goodbye, Mark."

The doorbell rings. My friends look crumpled, Jason especially in his pink linen shirt and white pants. "The longest fucking ride in my life," he says.

"You look lovely," I say to Gloria. This is true. She's my showpiece, almost as tall as me, and in heels, a bit taller. She wears heels even here; she somehow managed to find a pair of strappy sandals that look sexy but also safe enough to carry her through sand. But I doubt Gloria will cross the street to go to the beach. Even if she did, she would probably not get in the water unless it was for some higher purpose. There's no such thing as swimming in anything other than a pool when you're her age. When you're in your early forties, you're in the water because it's supposed to *do something* for you, whether it's burning calories or healing some ailment – a skin condition, imagined or not – or giving you a spiritual experience. An older woman almost never swims because it's fun. In contrast, a young girl swims because she swims – precisely because it's fun.

Yet Gloria looks as if she lives on the beach. Her hair is highlighted in perfect streaks of golden- and white-blond.

Perhaps because she's older than me, Gloria has never demanded anything of me. I'm grateful for this and reward her accordingly: an occasional sext to show her my commitment – *I can't stop thinking about biting the inside of your thighs* – and dinners and flowers; nothing too explicit, no jewellery. As I said, I enjoy taking her out in public – with her ex-model looks and tiny wrinkles, she seems not only attractive but also full of essence. Though most of it is vodka and bullshit.

"I made lunch," I say to Jason.

"Faggot lunch," Jason says, and shakes his head and gulps his beer as if he's forgotten he now reads magazines that tell him to eat faggot lunches and buy pink shirts. He's still a pig, the same pig I used to share a room with in school.

I serve Gloria vodka and soda. She doesn't eat lunches.

"Oh, you're just the nicest," she beams. In her early thirties, Gloria dated a Polish count who turned her onto vodka. The count was the only man she ever regretted not marrying. She wanted the title – she wanted the title so badly that when I first met her, she actually claimed to be a countess. Eventually she confessed: the fake titles and the fake orgasms, which, especially the latter, only improved our sex lives.

"To the beach house," says Gloria, sipping her vodka.

"To the beach house," I say, and turn to Jason.

"Why are the windows dimmed?" Jason asks. "To the beach house."

"He shoots porn in here. To the beach house," Gloria says in a tone that makes me feel proud for a moment, as if I had built this place myself. I like the easy, bored joke she made about the porn.

We spend the rest of our day joking and gossiping and sipping. We talk about Gloria's workplace. It's a PR firm that is now starting to get bigger deals: a small film festival and a small fashion week. Her firm, idiotically named after her – G-PR – has just hired a new slew of women, fresh out of PR school. Gloria says she no longer can tell the women apart. They all seem to be exactly the same age, though what age exactly she isn't sure: twenty-one? Twenty-seven?

"Plus they're all named Kayla or Krista or Karen, and they all have perfect skin and shiny hair, and this year they wear these indecent little outfits, I don't know, like teddies or something, I don't even know what those things are called but they're—"

"It's such a tease," Jason says. "See-through. But not."

"Exactly," Gloria says, and I want to tell her how impressed I am with her second joke, the one about all the K names and ages, but instead I say, "How's Kerry doing?"

Kerry is Gloria's right-hand girl, possibly the only girl at G-PR without the shiny locks and smooth skin. She vacationed with us in Hawaii and took care of Gloria's pet, a little ferret-like dog named Fifi. (Fun fact: it was the dog's name that inspired naming $isi.)

"Kerry's amazing. She was really helpful when Fifi—"

"Fifi was lovely," I say. "Pinch between your index finger and your thumb. It stops the tears," I squeeze Gloria's arm gently.

"She ate her own shit." Jason says exactly what I would like to actually say about the dog instead of what I just said.

"Fuck you." Gloria shakes her head. Her eyes are wet but no tears. "Kerry is taking over the London account soon, and then she can have my job."

"Nice," Jason says. "What are *you* going to do?"

"I'm going to start a magazine."

"Or a line of jewellery," I try to help, suddenly remembering some pillow talk Gloria and I had, maybe even during that trip to Hawaii, when Kerry stayed in a room next to the room where I fucked Gloria. I fucked Kerry in her room when Gloria was at the gym. It was very tiring.

Gloria thinks for a moment. "Or write a memoir."

"You should hire someone to write it for you. You're too busy and too pretty to be a writer," Jason says. He's trying to make up for the shit comment.

"Thanks. Maybe Guy knows someone. Do you know someone?"

"I do," I say. "Lots of someones who write, and who won't make it boring."

Gloria says, "You're mean. I'm not boring."

"You're not," Jason says. "You dated that count."

"You're not boring," I say.

"And I could always develop a cocaine addiction. Addicts are hot."

"It's been done, and it's not so hot," I say. $isi's face pops into my head.

Gloria says, "Or I could adopt."

Jason yawns, "It would have to be an Indian. Or a Jamaican. A little Rasta baby."

"Jason," Gloria hisses.

"Or it could be like the kids my mother used to tutor. Learning disabled," I say. Gloria's painted big toe pokes me gently in the side. Her feet are in my lap – her large, bony feet that have none of the sloppy softness of Dolores' feet, or at least what I guess Dolores' feet are like. I imagine chipped pink polish and some white fuzz on her toes, which she never thinks to shave. This thought produces a feeling of a sob coming on, somewhere in the bottom of my throat: oh, the tenderness of those imagined plump feet. I must be getting drunk.

Gloria talks some more about her job, something about how on Fridays there's always a little box of mint-green or pink or yellow macaroons from a place called Nadège, and there are little matching mint-green or pink or yellow flowers in a glass vase waiting for her on the desk. It's one of the new girls, a Kristen, who does this, and Gloria picks a macaroon every few hours and throws it into a plastic bag in her purse so that it looks like she's eating them.

"She's just trying to make you fat," Jason says.

"Oh my god, she *is*."

"It's passive aggressive. You should fire her," I say.

"There are laws about that," Gloria giggles.

"Laws schmaws." Jason burps and gets up, wavering a little as he walks to the fridge. He makes a lot of complicated noise, cursing something about how "these fucking ice cubes are wrong," which is the sort of thing that would bother Jason; he's straight but sometimes acts textbook gay, bitching about ice cubes being wrong.

I turn to Gloria and mouth *shall we?* meaning a fuck and a nap. It's getting late, almost three p.m. Soon we'll move into pre-dinner, and there's no way any of us will be able to survive it without a little rest.

I move Gloria's feet and pull her up. She sways and leans on me. "Bye-bye, Jason," she coos.

We go upstairs to the master bedroom, where we stand by the bed and undo my shirt first. Then Gloria's white-and-cream dress comes off. It floats like a little cloud, bouncing off the bed and settling on the wooden floor. And then we're in bed.

Her body is a combination of softness and muscle, the way her stomach barely ripples when she bends down, but when you touch it, it's soft, just like the rest of her body, which looks hard.

We don't kiss for long. Gloria is not much of a kisser, or maybe she used to be and is not anymore. I don't really care to kiss her anyway, but a gentleman should kiss; otherwise the lady might feel like a hooker. I heard somewhere hookers don't kiss. Jason said it wasn't true. In any case, when Gloria and I kiss, for a moment I taste her slightly tangy tongue, the spritzer, the vodka, and then she spits me out.

I move down to her neck and her breasts with nipples like tiny pink bulbs. I nudge with my nose under her breasts, feel the trace of moisture in the crease. I lick the trace of moisture, trying to get some salt out of it, but it's not really there; Gloria is too scrubbed. I'm talking years of scrubbing, not just this morning.

Her pussy is shaved. It's another soft/hard extension of the small planes that are her body. I cup the mound of it and slip my thumb between the folds. She's wet, the only part of Gloria that doesn't get scrubbed, or maybe is impossible to scrub, and that opens up, uncontrolled. She moans quietly. I rub the little nub inside it, which grows even slicker and harder under my finger.

I look at her face. She mouths *I want you.*

I'd prefer she was filthier, said something like *I want your cock* instead, but she just smiles expectantly as I roll a condom over my unaddressed cock and aim at the warm, pulsing hole.

I fuck it slowly first, and then faster. As I speed up, Gloria's legs go up and up until she locks them over my back. I lift her ass and pull her legs up to move them over my shoulders.

I close my eyes and imagine that I'm fucking someone else: Kerry, Gloria's assistant. I feel myself expand even more, sweetly, painfully.

I wait for Gloria to sync completely into our rhythm. It takes her a moment to get there, but I don't mind because the longer it takes her, the more Kerry she is. I hold her heavy, hard legs and pretend that they're heavy and soft, spongy almost, the way Kerry's legs would be.

"Now, baby?" I say.

Gloria moans in response, "Yes, yes, yes, now. Harder," and I fuck her harder and her pussy starts to spasm and squeeze me, *come on*, so I come, hard, inside Kerry, Gloria.

6

THE SATURDAY WITH GLORIA AND JASON IS MORE OR less a repetition of the Friday afternoon. Jason ventures out to the beach twice while Gloria and I fuck. I make two different salads and a puréed sweet potato soup for lunch; in the evening we drink and eat the leftovers. On Sunday, I wake up next to Gloria and my bed seems too small; I want her out of the bed. I feel like shouting at her to go, but I would never do that, shout at a woman.

I shake her and kiss her on the neck to wake her up.

The breakfast is eggs Benedict and silence. A table full of newspapers.

"I'm going to miss you, babe," Gloria says before they leave.

"I'm going to miss you, too," Jason says in a high-pitched voice.

"I'm going to miss *you*," I say back to him in my normal voice.

I'm impatient to go out and find Dolores, but it's no use this early in the day.

I watch the recap of the news on my computer. Amy Winehouse almost overdosed. A bomb in the Middle East killed forty people. A young woman got hit by a train and survived. Slow day. There are seventeen emails from $isi. I delete them all without reading.

I close my laptop. Go outside. The morning is cool and rainy, which is great weather for a run. Running, I try to focus on an image that will inspire me and make the inspiration stick, form into a girl, one girl, Dolores, but I'm all over the place mentally: $isi, Gloria, the pretty blond – the friend of Dolores' – a voice from the past, some girl's voice accusing me of something. Kerry or Kayla.

After the run, I work out in my basement, but my workout is as disastrous as my mind – I forget to count reps, I break a dial on my stationary bike; I say, "Fuck it," out loud and stop.

I take a shower, and after the shower I eat plain yogourt with muesli and drink a glass of freshly squeezed orange juice.

I take my dog for a walk. The beach is just starting to fill; the morning's dampness is still lingering in the air. It won't be damp for too long. I can sense the heat coming on. I walk along the road for a while, taking in the sights that I usually only get in a blur when I run first thing in the morning. There's a man-made waterfall to the east of my beach house. There are more beach houses to the west, and most of them are rentals. The fact that they're rentals is an ideal setup for me. I despise neighbourly relations, the expected pleasantries between people who happen to share a road and nothing else. The rentals are like musical chairs with a set of asses plopping down for a bit, a week or so, then disappearing to make room for a new set of asses.

Here it's mostly college kids. The biggest wave of them is during Spring Break, although we don't get full Daytona fuckery here. But it's all sex, humid air, sheeny skin, drunken vomit. Coconut oil and sugary drinks. The kids stumble by, flirting, pouncing on each other like lion cubs.

This early in the morning, the houses are still in disarray: wet shirts, wet towels, stacks of flip-flops and floatation devices and open coolers, empty cans of pop, puddles of fresh puke starting to dry, empty cartons of beer and bottles – bottles everywhere. Sometimes you see big, pink-faced, crusty-eyed boy cherubs rubbing their eyes on the too-bright porches. The girls who belong to these boys are sleeping inside. These are the pretty girls who get invited to beach houses with boys.

It is too early for the kind of girl that I'm looking for – a Dolores-girl. A Dolores-girl is also probably not at one of those beach houses. She's staying with her parents. Or maybe with friends whose parents own a house off the beach. She doesn't get invited to beach houses like these, anyway, and if she does, she thinks someone is playing a joke on her so she politely says *no*.

This early, a Dolores-girl is still slurping her fluorescent cereal, taking just one more bite of a muffin. She's trying to figure out which bright bathing suit to squeeze her doughy body into. She is in a dining room that is clean and bright and smells of Pine-Sol.

I know it seems like I make fun of a Dolores-girl by constantly referring to her pudginess and shapelessness and overall lack of contour, or even character, but the truth is just the opposite. I admire everything about a girl like this. I like how she thinks that nobody is looking at her. How she doesn't even make an effort, how she's already given up on her dream of becoming a model. Because let's face it, most girls her age would still be dreaming about being like Gloria, who at sixteen had modelled for an underwear label.

A Dolores-girl doesn't allow herself to think that she will run the world one day, be a model one day, if she only snaps out of it and fixes her nose and loses the sweet twenty pounds. She doesn't think she'll ever meet a prince and start a business of her own, a PR firm or a designer furniture store. She has realistic dreams, none of the delusions of the thousands of strung-out dieters out there who support modelling schools that are spreading like fungus all across the cities. A Dolores-girl dreams of men like me, but she doesn't believe men like me talk to girls like her.

And then I see her.

The promise of the second chin, and her perky nose, and the roots poking through the strands of blond hair. My Dolores. I say her name out loud. I actually enjoy how it rolls off my tongue – *Do-lo-res*. I remember now that this is Lolita's real name, the heroine in Nabokov's novel that I read as a child because it was supposed to be dirty, but it really wasn't. Dolores, the real one, with her sturdy trunk, is the opposite of Nabokov's lithe nymphet. In that, she is perfect.

My Dolores is sitting on a big towel with a book in her hand. The dog tugs at the end of his leash and gives a tiny, stifled woof. He probably remembers her smell, the way she stroked his head.

She looks up. Her eyes round and clear with bright irises and thick lashes. That mouth-breather mouth, pink lips parting in a daze that comes over her face. "Hi, Dog," she says.

"Dorothy?" I say, and give her a big smile.

"Oh, hi," she says, and looks up from making faces at the dog. She doesn't correct me about her name.

"What are you reading?" I point to the book.

"Oh. It's nothing. Just one of those stupid vampire books."

"Why is it stupid?"

"Oh, you know. Everyone's just like basically chasing each other with their fangs out and trying to not eat each other when they have...when they get together."

"A book? I haven't seen a real book since 2007," I say, and bend down to pick it up. "It's very interesting. I like the feel of it; it feels nice in the hand, solid. What do you do when the battery runs out? I don't see a USB slot anywhere."

"Yeah. I know," she says, and pretends to giggle, which is worse than if she just didn't do anything. I can't tell if this is because she found my joke lame or because she's so tense she can't get into it with me.

I put the book down, peek quickly at her toes: thick nails, no nail polish. Tiny thatches of blond hairs.

"So, how long are you staying for?" I say.

"Leaving Wednesday. It sucks, but Emily's parents won't let us stay on our own."

"Bummer. You're going to miss the tribute band for New Kids on the Block."

"You're kidding, right?" She giggles. I feel relief. Giggling is a must. And I don't know how to make jokes. It's painful for me to have to make them because I'm not good at them. And these aren't even jokes. It's true that there's going to be a tribute band for New Kids on the Block. There was a poster about the concert in the smoothie shack. I wonder if Dolores had noticed it, if she's indulging me – if she's indulging me, that means she's already hooked on me.

"I hate New Kids on the Block," she says. Even though it's impossible for her to sustain eye contact for more than a few seconds, we're talking with our eyes again. I tell her that I find her beautiful. She says she doesn't believe me. I tell her again, with my eyes. She, again, with hers says it can't be true. I need to keep this going.

"What kind of music do you listen to?"

"Why do you ask?" she asks, and I like this little spark of defiance or flirtation, I'm not sure which.

"I'm in the music business. I find music talent," I say.

"Would I know anybody you work with?" she asks.

"Sure. $isi and Charlie and before them some indie acts, like Ciraplex. Ciraplex is the name of an antidepressant. Clever, isn't it?"

Her mouth forms an almost perfect O. "Are you serious?"

"Sure." I bend down to pull the dog away from her – and to make physical contact for the first time. I let my fingers brush her arm very gently, just the tips of my fingers against her hot skin. "I can tell you more about my work if you're curious. Would you like to go for a walk?" I ask, breaking eye contact.

She gets up. She's not saying anything, probably trying to figure out what this is all about – me and my interest. A guy like me. It's going to take her some time to figure it all out, maybe the rest of her youth. Or maybe the rest of her life. I'm sure she's thinking that it's just too suspicious. She might be thinking that I'm going to skin her alive, make a hat out of her or leave her by the side of the road to bleed to death for fun. But she likes books about bloody things; maybe she hopes I'm a vampire.

I smile at her and she smiles back. "I usually just walk to there and then go back, is that okay with you?"

"Yes," she says, her voice small. She is perhaps imagining herself being bitten in the neck, perhaps picturing my face turning feline, fangs emerging from my mouth. We walk in silence for a while, just taking in the sights: the proudly jogging joggers, and the still-drunk-from-the-night-before teenage boys, and the guys in orange shirts with garbage bags who clean up the beach, and the young moms with uncombed hair sitting by their strollers or trying to contain their energetic toddlers, viciously smashing the sand.

I'm aware of Dolores through my body. My body reacts to her heat. I would like to put my nose in her hair, under her armpit, under her sweaty breast, but right now I'll have to do with what comes my way via the air. I can make out a cheap, fruity shampoo. A deodorant that's strong, so strong it must be a men's deodorant, the way it dominates all the other smells – sharp, with a violent tang of minty freshness. Underneath all this, I imagine Dolores smells sour and a little sweet, a little like a baby.

"It's beautiful, don't you think?" I point to the beach, the way the water looks dark against the white from the now-blaring sun, like an overexposed photograph.

She nods.

I talk about coming here a few years ago and falling in love with the way the sky and water looked, the morning contrasts and the evening's intense palate – both times of day so saturated with their own substance they seem heavy, velvet with colour.

I talk about how sometimes there is fog so strong it seems to linger on during the day. Even after the sun comes out, there are layers of haziness, like smoke.

I'm talking like I'm romantic. I'm better at talking like this than I am at making girls giggle.

Dolores finally gets the courage to ask me more about my work. I'm happy to oblige and tell her whatever I can about my temperamental muse, $isi. That's who interests Dolores most. She wants to know what $isi is like, and I'm not sure what to tell her.

Not in real life, $isi is a bubbly, feisty-yet-approachable pop star with hits like "Friday Night" and "Brokenhearted." Her favourite colour is red; she loves going to the movies; she's too busy with her music to get a pet, but she would love to get a rabbit one day. She bought her mother a house outside Vancouver, where she's originally from. She eats healthy, is not a night owl.

In real life, $isi is not a night owl because she's usually passed out from drinking before midnight. She's a smoker and a fucker of male groupies. She is trying to live up to her idol, Amy Winehouse. She hasn't been to the movies in years.

She'd probably prefer a rat to a rabbit, and she often talks about how she hates her mother. Privately, she says things like, "I want to pay someone to tell me how much I suck. Everyone says I'm so good. I'm surrounded by liars. I want to pay someone, like a dominatrix, to tell me I'm a worm."

Dolores wants to know what $isi's favourite food is.

I oblige: dark chocolate, ceviche (I explain ceviche), fruit (fermented fruit mostly, though I don't add this detail).

"Where did $isi go to school?"

"Where did *you* go to school?" I ask Dolores.

"A Catholic school. St. Mary's. My parents are Catholic, sort of. Well, my mother is, so I guess it was her idea. Now I'm at Brescia."

I don't know what Brescia is and Dolores explains that it's an all-girls college in London, Ontario. She is studying psychology there because she's interested in psychopaths, especially Paul Bernardo, who is Canadian, which is why it's awesome that she goes to school in Canada. What made him that way?

She goes on, "It's really frustrating because I can only take first-year courses, so that's, like, only general psychology. It's like they don't trust people to make their own choices and force them to take all this unnecessary crap because of some bullshit about students coming out well rounded, and it–"

To keep myself awake, I perform a couple of amusing chronological mind twisters: I was Dolores' age when Dolores was ten years old. That guy, Paul Bernardo, was my age when he killed a girl half his age. I was that girl's age at the time she was murdered. I'm not sure what all this adds up to.

I have to call $isi. My phone keeps pinging as her texts come through. I have to answer emails about the latest video. I have to make some arrangements to go see her in Montreal, where she's supposed to be doing a yoga retreat, but where she'll probably end up snorting lines with a DJ. All of this before I'm going to let myself have my afternoon nap, and before that, actually, have lunch, which today will include ginger potatoes with firm tofu in soy-garlic sauce with olive oil and an egg-yolk-mustard dressing on a dandelion salad.

***

We walk to my beach house now. Dolores admires it without speaking.

"I'm so glad we ran into each other," I say.

"Yeah. Me too. My book was really starting to depress me." The skin on her cheeks is peeling a little. Tiny flecks of white I would love to pick ever-so-gently with my tongue and swallow.

"I hate depressing stories," I say, even though I don't have the time to read much. At least not books.

"Isn't it the worst? Nobody can really be together like normal people. There's this vampire guy in the story, Albert – I should be reading something smart, like Dostoyevsky or something."

"Dostoyevsky is depressing. But you should give it a try."

"You think?"

"Yes. It's good to challenge yourself. Want to have dinner tonight? I'd like you to have dinner with me," I say.

She says nothing.

"You're quiet. Is that a no?"

"No. I mean, yes," she says, her voice shaking a little. She's trying to suspend any belief she's ever had about the things that don't happen to girls like her, things like meeting vampires or princes and living happily ever after. Magic.

"Great. See you tonight, Princess," I say. The nickname just pops into my head like that, perhaps because I am a nice, magical vampire prince.

7

FOR DINNER, I MAKE A CHILLED CAULIFLOWER VELOUTÉ AND kataifi pastry–crusted blue prawns with Romanesco broccoli and cilantro cream. This is the amuse-bouche, which I follow with some langoustines (wrapped in crispy potato and serrano ham) as an appetizer – I'm keeping to a relatively loose nautical theme.

The main is yellowfin tuna steak drizzled with some olive oil, paired with panisse and marinated anchovies.

For dessert, a Korean-grocery staple: black sesame ice cream accented with a dollop of green tea ice cream to offset the tacky sweetness with a nice bitter tang.

I serve some Pinot Grigio with the food, sparkling water on the side.

* * *

Dolores shows up right at six, and she's extremely pink. Her face is pink, her arms are pink, her dress is pink and her white shoes have pink shoelaces in them.

"You look nice. I love those shoelaces," I say, using the easiest trick in the book, my book, which is to compliment a girl on a detail in addition to the more expected, general flattery. In my experience, a woman remembers very well when you note the details: the unique piece of jewellery lost amid a stylish dress, the discreet scarf in the expanse of the more obvious coat, the way she does her hair (instead of just telling her she's got nice hair, say that you love it in a ponytail).

Dolores stares at her shoes and smiles.

The dining room is lit by candles. This, I hope, creates an ambience that evokes those fantasies of vampire boyfriends.

"Please sit down." I pull out the chair for her.

"This is amazing," she says, I'm not sure about what.

I serve our meal.

Dolores gets pinker with every course. "This is so amazing. So amazing."

There's quiet classical music coming from the speakers strategically placed on the walls – a slow, melancholic piano rainfall by Erik Satie, whom I talk about when Dolores asks. I tell her the story about Satie's twelve identical suits, found in the closet of a small room he lived in on the outskirts of Paris. I tell her about Satie carrying a small piano on his back as he travelled to the city to play in cafes, straining under the weight of his instrument and the weight of his largely undiscovered talent as he walked home in the night after his performances, quietly inserting himself back into his stark attic.

I move on to other subjects: the food we were just eating, how I got into the music business. How I was with $isi when she was nominated for her first Album of the Year award. How I had to console her afterwards because she lost to a gay cowboy – I give Dolores a PG-rated bullshit fable starring $isi and I going out for sorbet and seeing a flick with a funny actor in it to distract ourselves.

I ask Dolores about her family. She's not very forth-coming, says something about her father living in Mexico with a new wife, much younger than him. Her mother is dating a manager at the bank where she works. That's about it. "Nothing too exciting, everyone's cool, the end," Dolores says. She asks me about my family: are my parents still together?

"Yes," I say. (They share a nice plot at the cemetery, finally sleeping next to each other after years of separate bedrooms.)

"Do you have any brothers or sisters?"

I talk about my sister moving to Australia a few years ago.

"Why did she move there?"

"She met a guy."

"What is her husband like?"

I've never met him. I make up someone loosely based on the character from *Crocodile Dundee*, a rugged, snake-skin-wearing, lovable goof.

"How many kids do they have?"

"One. Sorry, two." I've never met them, either.

"Don't you miss them?" Dolores almost shouts.

"Very much so."

"What are their names?"

"Alice. And–"

I get up and grab the bottle of wine, muttering some-thing about it being almost finished. It isn't, but I can't remember the boy's name. My sister and I talk once a year, on my birthday.

I say, "Albert."

"Oh, I love that name," Dolores says softly.

"Because of the book you were reading. That was the name of the prince, right?"

"It's stupid."

"No, not stupid at all. You should never apologize for what you like. So, why do you like this Albert so much?"

"It's about conflict for me, I think? I mean, he wants to be with his soulmate, but he can't because he'll kill her if he tries to. So. He's very tortured? I mean it's kind of cheesy, but he's just–"

I sit down and fill her glass. I'm still trying to remember what my sister's boy is really called.

I ask Dolores more questions about Dolores. The intense attention is part of the seduction. And not only that: you have to make whatever she says seem interesting to her too: "What other *exciting* things are you up to this summer?"

"Not that exciting. Making up a calculus course because I have to have two maths before getting into statistics, and I only have one math and I'm not very good at it, so it's going to be difficult. It's going to be difficult to study in the summer, but what can you do. I will probably also–"

After a while we move to the living room, where Dolores giggles over the nudes in the Helmut Newton coffee-table book. She opens the Eric Kroll book *Fetish Girls* and slams it shut, giggles some more.

She drinks her wine. She drinks gin and tonic. I open more wine. I drink more wine.

She looks through my CD collection, asks me why I hold onto CDs even though there's iTunes, doesn't wait for an answer, puts on my *$isi Speaks* album and gets up to sway side to side while mouthing the words.

I concentrate on her pink shoelaces, swirling before my eyes. I usually don't drink this much.

Now she's sitting on the floor, right at my knees, leaning gently against my leg. I consider putting my hand on her head – think about how much I'd enjoy the soft feeling of her wispy hair – but I don't do that.

And again, she talks about the vampire prince from her book, Albert, and why she and her friends like him so much, how the boys their age could never measure up to someone so sophisticated and gentlemanly. All of a sudden, I recall my nephew's name: *Anthony*.

Dolores talks and talks. I remain passive, letting her direct the evening. I'm straining to stay awake and be Albert-like as I lounge on the couch with what I hope is an Albert-like look of fascination, longing and internal conflict.

Eventually, the evening ends. There's a kiss; a plan to meet the next day.

I sleep a drunken, dreamless sleep.

8

DOLORES IS WAITING BY THE SMOOTHIE SHACK. SHE'S WEARING a dress similar to the one she wore to dinner last night except this one is blue. I compliment her on the dress immediately, make sure to mention the cool pattern on it.

She blushes and says, "They're snowflakes, I think? Thank you so much."

The dress probably belongs to one of her friends – it's digging into the skin above her breasts. It's too tight in the back as well, making angry red rows when she moves, possibly feeling my eyes there. It's not her discomfort that excites me (though perhaps there's a little bit of that too) but how impossible it is for Dolores to *get it right*.

She bends down to pet Dog.

I watch her back for a moment, fascinated by the straps but also feeling a little impatient. I'm not at my calmest this morning thanks to idiot $isi and her middle-of-the-night tears. And my workouts continue to go badly, so I'm not in my usual easy-flow state of mind. I try to remember the cognitive exercises I taught myself – not to listen to negative thoughts, to think of neutral topics (nature, fashion, travel) or imagine a garden from my childhood – but instead I get caught in every dark place in my mind. In that state, neutral topics become troublesome: *travel* turns to thinking about the Sudan; *nature* reminds me of a rabid dog in my childhood; *fashion* conjures images of $isi's nipple slips and bad haircuts.

Dolores must be picking up on my mood because she's quiet, contained – much more contained than she was last night when she went as far as to show me her favourite illustrators on DeviantArt (vampires, girls with skull masks on their tattooed faces, ghostly figures with dresses turning into leaves blown away by the wind) and hipster videos on YouTube (big girls in little-girl dresses talking to clouds, stop-frame animation about a girl's hang-ups regarding her giant nose, men using their toddlers as weights).

"I've had a bad morning, I apologize, I'm feeling unwell," I tell Dolores, with knowledge that this kind of sharing, admitting to my weakness, is also a great opportunity for her to feel useful and therefore in power, which may, hopefully, even out our balance, at least momentarily, and allow me to gain a bit more of her trust, make the further, necessary moves.

"Oh, don't apologize. It's totally okay," Dolores says. "Anything I can do?"

I pull her close and hold her against my body. I don't say anything.

She stiffens in my arms, looks up. Her round eyes get even rounder.

Last night's kiss was a kiss of clinking teeth and too much fumbling on her part when it was time to go: many extra gestures (smoothing her hair, shaking hand, touching my arm and flinching as if it burned) and some more babbling.

Now, I lift her chin up. She opens her mouth. This time it's much better, technically, despite the fact that her mouth is trembling slightly and her tongue goes in circles then stops abruptly. But she could bite my tongue and it would be fine – she's wonderful in her idiocy. Her hands rest stiffly on my waist. As the kiss goes on, the hands move equally stiffly until they finally meet in the middle. I run my fingers over the ridges in her skin where the straps of her dress are digging in.

When I finally pull away, she lets out a loud sigh. She's falling in love with me. This thought, as soon as it forms itself, does something to the anxiety I've been feeling all morning. It melts it, pushes its bile back down. I feel better. In my gratitude, I pull her toward me again and kiss her again, this time harder, with my tongue pushing hers, biting ever so slightly on her lower lip, like Albert the vampire would do. This kiss is short. She is left breathing a little too fast when I break it.

We walk back, mostly in silence. I invite her over for lunch later, and of course she accepts.

We kiss again. Same confused tongue.

"See you soon, Princess," I say.

"Okay. Bye." She turns around.

I know she knows I'm watching her now because I notice her struggling to swing her hips (sexily?) and straighten out her feet. Her back is so stiff I just know that she's killing herself not to turn around and check if I'm looking.

* * *

Fifteen minutes before lunch, I make buttermilk pancakes with asparagus in a classic white sauce. I serve it hot. Dolores is not late. I don't have the focus to pay close attention to her outfit because the sauce has just been prepared and the stalks of asparagus are seconds away from losing their firmness and heat. I serve the pancakes with the vegetable and sauce right away. The pancakes are perfectly fluffy.

During lunch, Dolores asks me to make her a gin and tonic. She drinks it fast and I wonder if she may be an alcoholic. Why not? She's old enough. $isi became a drunk when she was about her age or younger. Dolores' potential alcoholism seems to be confirmed when she asks for another gin and tonic before lunch is over.

"It's delicious," she says. "The sauce."

"It's a very simple recipe. I'm happy to teach you," I say. I realize that I haven't come up with any way to amuse her until enough time passes to make a move. Perhaps a cooking lesson will do. I say, "We could make the sauce now. We'll recreate."

She blushes. "Oh, I don't know."

Her speech is not slurred. I can't be sure the alcohol got to her considering her weight. She stares at her plate.

"What is it, Princess?"

"I want to have sex with you," she says quietly.

"Come again?"

"I don't want to cook. I want to have sex with you," she says, sounding a little angry. But it's not anger. It looks more like determination. She's still not looking at me. A vein pulses in her temple. I haven't noticed that vein before. It will get more prominent with age unless her face balloons from obesity.

"Are you feeling drunk?" I say. I prefer not to have sex with someone who's drunk, especially a younger girl.

"A little. But I only drank because I had to get the nerve to say it to you, and now I've said it." She burps. "I'm sorry," she says.

"Oh, no, that's a huge turn-on, actually," I say, and she fake-laughs. "I like confident girls like you," I say.

I take her face in my hands and kiss her on the forehead. Then I lead her upstairs to the master bedroom, which has its own balcony overlooking the dinky man-made waterfall, which makes Dolores squeal. "You're so lucky!" She runs to the balcony and takes off her shirt.

"Princess." I gently pull her away from the balcony, turn her around to have a look at her breasts. They are larger and shapelier than I thought they would be. She'll do well with prospective sexual partners if she chooses to showcase this feature. Some men are really into breasts; they will even put breasts above a good-looking face or intellect. There's no way I could ever tell her this without sounding terribly insensitive, but I wish I could. It's useful information.

"You have the most beautiful breasts," I say, hoping she'll stick that in her memory vault and use it in the future, whenever she doubts there's something about her that could be interesting to look at. That's all I can do.

I take the rest of her clothes off and push her gently onto the bed. I take in the very soft body, the trimmed dark bush, the dark moles on her belly. "You are so beautiful, so beautiful," I tell her.

"Am not," she says softly, and I say, "Be quiet, Princess."

She reaches out and touches my chest with excited hands. She pushes my hand away when I try to touch her back. "No," she snaps. I know that her boldness is partly due to drunkenness, and I enjoy it even though I prefer to be in control. I let her fingers reach my nipples to tweak them. Then she nervously reaches for my dick. I kneel over her. I lock my eyes with hers. I encourage her gently: "That's good, that's perfect."

Her grip is weak, but it does the job relatively well. Well enough to make me ask her to stop at one point. I kiss her down her wobbly stomach, rut with my nose between the hot, wet folds of her pussy. Eventually, I start fucking her. Her eyes are on me, searching and reaching out to mine. She is quiet.

I turn her over. I reach down underneath her to stroke her as I slowly go at her. I stroke her for a long time and eventually this makes her come – she squeals and whines. She is noisy, finally, after almost-silent intercourse.

I pull out and slip off the condom and flip her onto her back again and spray all over her belly.

When I open my eyes, she's looking at me, smiling. She says she loves – me or *it*, I can't hear clearly. I lie down beside her, pull her close and say, "Mmm." Her head smells of coconut; I fall asleep with my nose buried in her hair.

9

THE HOURS I SPEND WITH DOLORES ARE SIMILAR TO WHAT
it was like with $isi. They look nothing alike, but when I look
at Dolores, it's like $isi is superimposed over her, and I have
to keep doing mental double takes. Maybe it's something
in their gestures. Or maybe the way they both eat sloppily.
Or the constant chatter – first childhood crush, first pet,
first serious injury, how much textbooks cost, coming back
here for Spring Break, how gross ham is but how delicious
bacon is, what she thinks of – These are the sorts of inane
tidbits $isi has offered before, just as frantically, to cover
her nervousness over being with me.

Dolores and I part for a few hours, then we have another
dinner – takeout Thai, which I think is disgusting but which
she loves.

Later, we fuck again. She stays overnight. In the morning
we eat grapefruit for breakfast and a smoothie made out

of banana, strawberry, avocado and apple juice not from concentrate. Dolores is silent in a loud, tragic way, and I'm silent, too, because I'm reading a newspaper.

After breakfast, she asks if I will drive her to the bus station in the afternoon. She is leaving today. I will never see her again. I like the thought of literally driving her away from me. I wish it was this easy with $isi, or I wish there was a way to surgically correct $isi's brain so that whatever it is about me that got stuck in there could be removed like a tumour. I'd pay for the surgery. Everyone would benefit.

Dolores says, "I know you said not to get upset, but I can't help it? This was really—"

I hold her head against my chest and stroke her hair. Whatever she's saying, I can't make out a thing.

* * *

Later on, I pick her up after lunch at her friend's parents' house, somewhere on the outskirts of the beach village where the families with kids live. In contrast to what you see around my beach house, the street here is quiet, full of trimmed bushes and little gardens; no passed-out half-dressed teenagers on porches.

The house where Dolores is staying is a bungalow with a smaller, equally ugly building attached to it that bears a nameplate reading *Teenagers' House*. There's a sign in front of the bungalow with a big *SOLD* on it.

Dolores and her friends come out of the Teenagers' House with bags as soon as I pull into the driveway.

Dolores runs up and throws her arms around my neck. She tries to slip her tongue into my mouth, but I cut her off, even though I understand that she's doing this partly for show.

Her eyes widen.

I quickly kiss her on the cheek to not make a scene.

The girls load into the car. Dolores sits in the front. The pretty blond, Kelly, and the brunette with glasses sit in the back.

"Cool ride," Kelly says.

She's right. It is a cool ride. Only a year ago I drove a little Acura that I had to part with because it made me look like I was afraid to grow up. Like I was a bro. A knapsack-filled-with-condoms-in-the-backseat kind of bro. I sold the car to Jason and he immediately reclined the front seat "so the chick has no choice but to lie down when you drive her," he said. He planned to have a lot of sex in that car with chicks he'd meet online. They could smell it; it would increase his chances if a girl got in his car and it smelled like it'd been fucked in, he told me. It was one of his PUA wisdoms.

I don't own cars to fuck in them. I drive my cars. So I bought the Infiniti G37 Cabrio. To drive it. A black convertible, butterscotch leather interior. Three-twenty-five horsepower V6. Six-speed, manual shift. I could have gone for the seven-speed automatic transmission with paddle shifters, but women like to see you shift gears. It's the crudest association, your hands on that stick, handling it.

The car came with a seven-piece Bose stereo system with twelve-inch woofers in the rear. It is roomy enough to transport three women comfortably. It is a cool ride; Kelly is absolutely right.

Dolores starts fiddling with the stereo as soon as we get on the road. "Can I play them the song? The one Yumiko is singing. It's so good."

She means my Japanese-American band, Charlie, and the song I hope will be in the soundtrack in a movie about a teenager who stalks another teenager. The song is something that the band hasn't tried before. It's almost entirely electronic: catchy kick drums, Auto-Tuned vocals and two drops – the first gentle and the second one faster, filthier and deeper. The lyrics are partly Japanese.

Dolores doesn't wait for me to answer – such are the entitlements of a girlfriend – and the song *boom-bah-booms* out of the speaker, filling the car with its sexy, velvet intro: *Anata o aishitai, demo anata wa itte shimatta. Anata ga inakute sugoku sabishii. Ikanai de hoshii. Soba ni ite hoshii. Mou ichido anata o aisasete kudasai.*

I think of Yumiko, the girl who came into the studio to sing this part, a big-eyed anime character. She seemed flat-chested like a boy, but maybe it was the tight corset top she was wearing. During the break, I heard two sound guys talk about the long white socks she wore – one of the guys groaned that the socks were "obscene." He said he wanted to take her home and – he didn't finish. His friend told him to shut up. They were young guys, possibly still trying to figure out their sexuality.

The socks *were* obscene. In the best possible way.

The socks' boyfriend was waiting for her at the hotel, or so she said when I invited her for a drink after the recording.

"No problem," I said, and shook her hand.

Later, it turned out her breasts were indeed tiny; deliciously tiny, a dollop of cream topped with pink nipple. Straight black pubic hair. The socks stayed on as requested.

"Yumiko? She usually plays bass, doesn't she?" says the brunette.

"She pretends to play bass," I say.

"What do you mean?"

"They're all singers, actually," I say. "It was just an idea to market them this way, as a band."

"So it's a lie?" Dolores says, so loudly I would actually call it shouting.

"No, not a lie. It just made more sense to go in that direction. They can play musical instruments. Just not really well. You don't need to play them very well anyway. Especially bass."

Kelly says, "Aren't you worried we're going to tell people?"

"And?"

"I don't know. That the news will spread that it's all a marketing ploy."

"You don't actually believe that there's anything left out in the entertainment world that isn't a marketing ploy, do you?"

Dolores says, "Yes, but–"

"There are some independent acts that get through, it's true. But we snatch them up and that's the end of that," I say, and pretend-laugh to indicate that I'm joking but maybe not.

"This is why Amy Winehouse will die for sure," says Kelly, darkly.

"Who gives a fuck?" says the brunette, and I look in the mirror again, and she meets my eyes without blinking. I smile in a friendly way, but the eyes remain unmoving, watchful.

"Everything okay?" I say.

Kelly says, "The song's really great anyway. Dolores was going on about it, but we were, like, totally distracted."

"We were asking her too many questions about what type of fuck you are," the brunette says.

"Em!"

The brunette's dark eyes in the mirror narrow slightly. Dolores told me that she and Em are best friends.

Em doesn't seem to have any of Dolores' and Kelly's bubbliness; she looks like she is only capable of scowling. I know women in their thirties whose lips have a permanent downward skew from this kind of repeated muscle arrangement. You find out later, face to face on a pillow, they used to be Goths or drug addicts or runaways – or all three – in their younger years. Dissatisfaction takes its toll. I predict Em's face will to go the downward route. Dolores had been unable to explain what she and Em have in common other than that they grew up together. Em berates her, tells her to exercise. Women are often friends with other women they hate. I don't know why.

"Don't mind her. Em's just hormonal," says Kelly. "And she's breaking up with her boyfriend when she gets back, so—"

Em rolls her eyes. "Shut it, Kels."

"Well, you are."

"Why is that?" I say.

"Because he doesn't deserve her?" Dolores' voice is small.

"Did he cheat on you?" I don't look in the mirror.

Kelly sighs, "No. He's just—"

"He's weak," Em says, and I wonder what that means to her. But I'm not really interested in finding out; I'd prefer to be talking about Charlie's potential hit song, so I gently bring us back to that topic, ask what they think again.

"I thought it was great. I'd buy it for sure. I love the singing in it too, but it's different than their usual stuff. I can't tell with Korean," says Kelly.

"Japanese. Her name is Yumiko," Dolores says in an offended tone.

"It doesn't work for me," Em says. I look in the mirror again but she's looking down. Probably texting.

Dolores says nothing. She must be dealing with a lot of big feelings right now.

After everyone unloads and proceeds toward the bus station, the two other girls walk ahead of us, faster, to give me and Dolores some space. Dolores hands me a letter, which I'm sure contains fifteen different suggestions on how to contact her, as well as some declarations of love and devotion. It's not the first letter like this I've received.

Dolores throws her arms around my neck. This time, I kiss her properly, with tongue. Then Em or Kelly pulls her away and they all get on the bus and I wave once and walk away, completely exhausted by it all.

* * *

In the letter, there's some confusing poem about love – something about the river Kiang and meeting at Cho-fu-Sa.

There's a Twitter handle, Facebook account, even a LinkedIn address carefully handwritten, which I appreciate more than anything – it's impossible to find anyone under the age of twenty who is able to handwrite anymore.

For my part, I've given Dolores a printout with numbers and email addresses that are missing one crucial letter or have the number one instead of a seven and so on.

I know that it's almost impossible to hide in the world anymore, and that young women like Dolores make online stalking their pastime, but it's relatively hard to find me out there. Besides, even plain girls who meet princes get distracted – by math, by a boy with a guitar, by becoming passionate about saving pets, etcetera.

I make a nice memory, but my silence makes it quickly obvious that they were right about their instincts that it was too good to be true. And the fake numbers and so on prove it. There was no mistake.

Furthermore, after years of being "accidentally" found online and a few times in real life by wannabe rock stars, I have some firewalls in place. I have fake Facebook profiles. I have hired a student from Mexico to monitor my social media presence and insert content into places where I supposedly hang out. He links to interesting articles on Facebook that are never about politics, religion or sex. He comments on other people's non-sexual, apolitical, non-religious posts – usually animals and babies and optical illusions. Simple pronouncements such as *Excellent!* I don't mind the brevity – his English is limited; the brevity is perfect. Occasionally he posts about something serious, like the environment – everybody loves the environment – or healthy eating (but nothing controversial, like gluten). I send him the links to articles.

On my actual Facebook account, I only post pictures of the meals I make if I'm particularly proud of them. Barely any comments. Recently I've asked the student from Mexico to ask other students from Mexico for comments on these photos. It's bizarre to me that nobody cares about beautifully prepared food.

I have no idea what memory Dolores will leave. For now, all I've got of her is the creamy belly and round back, the red marks from her tight clothes, the open-mouthed look, the curl on her neck when she pulled her hair into a ponytail. The smell of coconut and men's deodorant. There's also the windmill tongue and her shuffle-walk.

10

AFTER I SLEEP FOR TWELVE HOURS AND WAKE UP FEELING five years younger, I sit down with a glass of freshly squeezed orange juice and devise a workout plan for the next few weeks. My workout chaos persists. It's time to fix that.

I open a new document and start typing the number of reps and suggested successions that'll let me get back on track. I consider calling my former personal trainer to ask him about high-interval training. I wonder if it could be an improvement on my cardio routine.

I quickly change my mind about calling him. It's possible he's not with his girlfriend anymore, but if he is, who knows what kinds of things have been confessed? There was only that one time. It was quick, efficient, exactly like a workout. It was in their apartment with extremely white walls, the gym-like smell of disinfectant in the air. It involved about forty push-ups on my part, and after I got dressed, I ran an impressive sprint worthy of high-interval training because my personal trainer, her boyfriend, was buzzing the intercom downstairs.

It was stupid of me. He was a very good personal trainer.

* * *

After I'm done typing out my workout plan, I move on to food. I check my Excel files for detailed menus worked out by the nutritionist I hired last year. Our relationship is the most perfect relationship in my life: he emails me the plans every quarter and I enter my credit card number.

There are at least four weeks of meals left. I phone my food-delivery guy and read him my new grocery list over the phone. He no longer snickers about the food items I ask for or tries to tell me about his life involving pickup trucks and blonds. Once he finally realized I don't care, our relationship became *almost* perfect: me reading out the ingredients and amounts, and him not saying anything until I say, "That is all."

I would love to be able to do this with Gloria one day: just announce whatever sexual fancy strikes me at the moment. As it is right now, I first, always, have to listen to stories about her PR firm, her sister's family life or the benefits of using dry shampoo. Only after she vomits it all out, she might acknowledge my lips brushing against her neck, my hand pressing her hand against my hard-on.

I'm not being entirely fair. I enjoy Gloria's company. And, as I mentioned, she's great to take out in public. Plus, as far as girlfriends go, she's close to perfect. I've never even seen her cry.

* * *

I stay at the beach house for the next three weeks. There's nothing to do in Toronto, where I spend my winters. Gloria is away in Bali with her sister, and $isi is completing another short-term rehab stint. That's fine. I can be anywhere, there's no rush to leave and the weather is nice.

I work on the beach house, cleaning it throughout, making it ready for the next visitor. I'm renting the place to Jason when he comes back in September. I write out rules for him as soon as we make the arrangements. One of the rules is: *No meth in the house. Or outside of the house. No meth ever.*

Jason has tracked down his ex and he's thinking of bringing her here. "She needs to be in a non-confrontational environment," he says on the phone. He sounds pathetic. His words rush into one another as he tells me how he won't tolerate any bullshit anymore and how much the ex has changed since the last time they were together. Things are going to work out.

Except that that's not going to be the case.

I don't say this to Jason. I found out a long time ago that there's no point in talking people out of stupid things they want to do. Most of us never mature past the age of four. I tell him I hope it works out.

"What do you mean, *you hope*? Of course it'll work out," Jason says.

"I liked you better when you were a PUA," I say. "Do you remember staying at my place with your knapsack and all you had inside were rubbers?"

"I don't remember that."

"Okay. Send me the name of your trainer."

We hang up.

Despite my stoicism on the phone, internally I am disturbed. I have to come up with a couple of calming thoughts (the nice run this morning, last night's first successful soufflé of the season) to quell the anxiety and ignore the image of the beach house destroyed in some druggy rage – or worse, turned into a meth den.

I think about how Jason is the opposite of me. He falls for girls who don't match him. He pines after strippers and waitresses and girls who ruffle his hair like he's a puppy or a younger brother. Girls with low self-esteem but high self-regard. Girls who fuck him because they had a fight with their boyfriend or girls who are waiting for the guy who doesn't want to commit to call back. Jason pines after the kind of girls I could easily have. Back in university, I would get middle-of-the-night emails, sloppy drunken come-ons from his girlfriends at parties – *I know there's something between us, I've always thought you were so handsome* – as if I needed to be told that, as if that were some kind of a prize for me, Jason's girlfriend.

I wish there was something I could do or say to rescue Jason from his taste, but I know he's delusional. He represents the worst-case scenario of what may happen to some of my conquests: chasing after people who are like me for the rest of their lives, or expecting their actual lovers to measure up to a fantasy.

So it is not my place to say anything to Jason about his tastes and delusions. And I have to admit, it's somewhat entertaining to watch him struggle so much in the name of desire. It's foreign to me, his struggle.

***

After the beach house is cleaned and tidied up, I spend most of my time taking Dog for long walks and watching television.

I look at girls on the beach, taking in all the imperfections. I don't approach anyone and no one approaches me. I keep my distance. But I see everything. I revel in the bellies and thighs of the big girls as much as the gawky flatness of the skinny ones and the shapelessness of those who are neither. I can smell them without smelling them, and many of them smell like Dolores – and $isi too – milk and spit and chemical sweetness, sun and sand. Sometimes there's a boyfriend or boys around those girls, and sometimes as I fuck a girl in my mind, I imagine myself to be one of those boys, my flat hand slapping her sloppy ass, *Good girl.*

One morning, I notice a couple on the beach. I order Dog to sit, and we sit in the shadow of the dunes, watching. They are splayed out in camping chairs beside a big blue cooler, most likely filled with beer for him and chips for her. The guy is pale and skinny with a pregnant belly and a haircut that hasn't seen a decent shape since childhood. The girl is not skinny. She is rectangle-like in a one-piece bathing suit with cutouts meant to suggest curves. It fails: the bottom is cupping her flat ass so that the beginning of her crack is visible above it. Her hair hangs like a cheap curtain, convulsing here and there in random waves of yellow streaks.

As she gets up, it's obvious that she's not terribly confident about the bathing suit. This is what intrigues me – the way she attempts to hide inside it, trying to make it seem like no big deal, as if the suit hasn't been designed to specifically accentuate her sexiness. I imagine a scene from whatever horrible town they're from: an over-lit change room at Target, some girlfriend of hers encouraging her to get this suit *because it would be a crime not to since it makes you look so totally, like, hot.*

I watch the girl shuffle through the sand and into the water, submerging carefully, lifelessly. She stays in the water for a short time, as if this was a duty she had to perform, then comes out dripping wet, walking with her eyes cast down. My hard-on pushes against my shorts. Dog stirs beside me, probably sensing my excitement, probably mistaking it for the desire to get going.

As the sun comes out from behind a cloud, for a split moment, the black contours of the bathing suit are all I see, the girl's white rectangular shape washed out in the light and white sand. In the light, she becomes the impossibly, cartoonishly defined woman-body that the suit promised she would be. So funny. I snap out of my little fantasy of walking up to her, bending her over the blue cooler and having her right there in front of the boyfriend.

I suddenly find the beach oppressive, as if the ruined illusion of the girl actually, physically burst inside me, hurled me toward some sort of limit I had and broke through, exposing me to my surroundings. I become aware of how the beach crowd resembles a mob, the people growing sweaty and tense from the sun. They are frying their brains right out in the open, shovelling junk food into their endless mouths, the shouty radio commercials everywhere. Everyone is too fat or too weak or too crazy to escape, at least till the evening, when it gets cooler.

"Let's go," I say to Dog, and we walk on, both of us done with the beach and ready to go home, back to prepare for winter in Toronto. I motivate myself to walk faster. I conjure a fantasy of being followed by a mob of hungry fatsos, snapping their jaws behind me like I'm a bag of chips. I don't turn around.

11

NOTHING HAPPENS FOR ALMOST A WEEK AFTER I GET BACK
and then, in less than twenty-four hours, there are twenty-
one emails from Dolores in my professional email inbox at
my agency. Some of the subject lines are: *Hello, Its* [sic.]
just me!, *At last* [sic.] *let me know if your* [sic.] *alive, I cant*
[sic.] *believe it* and *Read this 1 before the last 1 PLS!!!!*
[sic. sic. sic.]

I fire my remote Mexican assistant for not monitoring
my professional email account diligently enough. I don't
spend a lot of energy on trying to figure out how she got my
email address. I'm no match for an eager young woman who
grew up thinking psychopathic behaviour such as stalking
is nothing more than your right to keep in touch.

I'm alarmed by how much such a little thing disturbs
me. It's as if something has entered my home, a dark presence like a ghost. On the night of the emails, I am unable
to sleep, so I leave my apartment and walk around the city

with Dog for hours until we both get tired and go back and pass out on the couch.

Before passing out, I block Dolores' email and send an email blast to my contacts about updating my address. I hire a more expensive Mexican assistant to monitor my email account.

I disable my Twitter and my Facebook page.

* * *

I book a weekend in Montreal to meet with $isi, who is back from rehab, which she, predictably, cut short because she was not allowed to use her new iPhone. I refuse to go to her hotel, and this puts her in a bad mood right away. I don't justify my refusal with anything other than reminding her that this is a professional meeting, not a personal one. She snorts. "Of course it's professional. My manager is coming."

"Speaking of Mark, he's gotten a little chubby, no?" I say.

$isi hangs up on me.

I send her a text with the hotel address and the time. She doesn't text back.

Not texting me back is intentional. It makes me pace across the lobby until a conventionally pretty (symmetrical, straight-haired) girl in a slick black hotel uniform clicks across the marble floor and asks if I'd like to take a seat at the bar. I take a seat at the bar and order a drink.

* * *

$isi walks in alone. She's always been small, but now she looks crushed under the weight of her massive sunglasses, the heavy-looking hardware that doubles as a necklace and the big white-and-black raccoon hair. She's wobbly in Lucite stripper platforms. When she sits down at the bar, she shakes once, briefly, like an old lady – I want to put my hand on her shoulder to steady her, but I don't want her to misread the signal.

She takes off her sunglasses to show me her makeup – a uniform black smudge across her face where her eyes are. "How is this even Montreal? I fucking hate that I can't smoke in here," she says.

"How are you?"

She looks at me, her green eyes electric against the black.

"I'm good," I say. "Thanks for asking. Here's the list with all the venues, times and dates, as well as some contact numbers and other information. I want you to look at this printout with me here so that I can actually witness you acknowledging it."

"Whatever."

"This has been going on for too long."

She looks up. "You know what you are? You're practically a pedophile. I've been reading about men like you. You sleep with young chicks like me because we won't confront you and because we don't know any better."

I smile at the pretty hotel girl as she walks by. She smiles back.

"$isi, please." I use the most caring yet detached tone I can manage. "If I hear a reference to our sleeping together ever again, I'm going to spread the word that you are consistently difficult. I know some people will still be eager to work with you, but I will also see to it that we release some of your demo tapes. You won't need to pay a dominatrix anymore to tell you that you suck, that you're a worm. So, be polite."

Most of what I say is bullshit. $isi can easily find another good agent, but she's young and stupid and weak right now, battling all her addictions, getting caught necking with pimply-faced groupies in skid row bathrooms, rolling and smoking joints and eating at McDonald's. I know there's an old video, too, of her smoking what looks like a glass pipe, and there's a recording of a nasty message she left her assistant. I hope she recalls all of this as clearly as I do right now. "I hate being so harsh, $isi," I say. "But like a good parent, I sometimes have to be. Tough love. I like the new look, by the way. The hair."

"So you my daddy now?"

"Your hair really suits you."

"It's just hair."

"It looks nice."

$isi stretches her mouth into an unsuccessful smile. She looks like a demon. "Daddy. So. Are you still with that old lady?" she says.

I don't answer. Gloria is coming back from Bali soon, and it would be nice to see her for a drama-free weekend when I feel like being around people again.

"Hello," Mark says somewhere behind me. As always, he is sweating slightly, as if he ran here. Maybe he did run here. He can be calm on the phone, but he's one of those people who looks like he's got a live monkey attached to him, the way he's always crumpled and bug-eyed.

He gives $isi a close squeeze, molesting her thin back for a second too long, and I wonder if they've slept together. Maybe to get back at me, hoping that I'd care. She doesn't hug him back, and he stands awkwardly next to our bar stools until I suggest we all sit at one of the tables and move on with our meeting.

"You've lost some weight, Mark," I say.

"Thanks," he says. "I don't think so."

"No, definitely," I say.

"Yoga," he says, shyly.

"I love yoga," I say.

As we walk away from the bar, $isi moves closer to me and quickly whispers in my ear, "I hate you so much," which would be a great title for a new song she could write. I make a mental note to bring that up in our meeting. She leaves her vodka, untouched, on the bar.

* * *

$isi comes back to my hotel in the middle of the night. She rings me from the lobby. She's sitting in a chair, and her face is small, makeup-free. She looks older and younger than herself, somehow, at the same time. I don't know which drug did this to her, or if it's just drunkenness.

She sees me and gets up, stumbling a bit. There it is again: that jerkiness to her movement, as if someone were pulling on strings. "I had some time to think about things."

"Drink about things?"

"Now that's a brilliant dad joke!"

"$isi, you're tired. Let's get you in bed."

"Great idea. Let's get me in bed."

"Wait here." I go up to the front desk to ask for a separate room for her. I don't have any other ideas this late at night. I want to go back to bed.

"Is she okay? Would you like me to call someone?" the desk girl says. I don't know if she's the same girl as before. Same hair, same uniform. Same pretty.

"She's very tired. She travelled and lost her luggage. We're looking into it," I say.

The girl smiles. I sign the bill. "Let me know if there's anything else," she says. *Suck my dick.* I smile and shake my head. "No, that's all. Thank you."

I pull $isi to her feet and we walk, slowly, jerkily, toward the elevator. "I'm firing you," she says.

"Okay. We'll talk tomorrow."

We get on the elevator. Our image is a blur in the smoky glass. She looks like a thing someone squiggled. I drag-walk her to her room. She immediately curls up in the large reading chair.

I grab a blanket to put over her, but she pushes it down and mumbles something about being too hot. I walk back to my room.

I fall into my bed, fall asleep immediately and dream of being chased by a bear, then drowning in the pond where I try to hide from it.

12

THE NEXT MORNING, I ORDER ROOM SERVICE, AND A YOUNG man shows up wheeling a little cart with my breakfast on it. I've ordered a grapefruit and a Montreal bagel with cream cheese, and fresh orange juice and coffee. The bagel is too dry, the cream cheese cold and hard but with a film of grease.

After breakfast, I walk over to $isi's room and knock on her door; no one answers. I slip the key card in the slot and walk inside. The bed hasn't been slept in. I notice $isi on the floor, on the other side of the bed, by the window. She's on her back. She is very white with a punch of red for lips. Right away, I picture a gurney with her tiny form laid out on it being wheeled out of the hotel. The camera flashes, the microphones, Mark showing up sweaty and crazed (his invisible monkey pinching him frantically), blubbering.

I crouch down to see her. She's breathing. There's a wet spot underneath her. I bend down to smell it. Urine.

"I fell out of the bed," she croaks and opens her eyes.

My relief is quickly followed by a twinge of disappointment. Dead rock stars can bring in a lot of revenue. I may not care that much about money, but I am not completely indifferent to it.

"I fall out of bed all the time. There's something wrong with me."

"Is it drugs?"

"It's not fucking drugs. I'm done with that. I don't even drink now," she sighs. She closes her eyes.

I bend down to lift her. There's a feeling to her – a feeling I remember from when I was a child visiting my dying grandmother. It was the way her hands were, like her bones were spilled matches, like whatever she was had died a long time ago. This is what $isi feels like, like she's not quite there.

I gently lower her onto the bed. She's not saying anything. I have a hard time believing that I fucked this little body; that I opened it, and it was wet and soft and full of redness and life.

* * *

Mark shows up with his assistant, a hipster with a T-shirt advertising *Camp Abilities 1975*. They talk in loud whispers, asking me what happened, looking at the stain of pee, hovering above $isi to listen to her steady, strong breath. It is decided that they will take her to the emergency room. Some phone calls have to be made to arrange this as discreetly as possible.

I know that it will still get out to the press, so we call Piglet/Jennifer to update her on everything and make sure she's got some answers ready when the news gets out. She wants to know what $isi has taken to get so ill, but none of us has any idea.

"It just looks like she's really, really tired," Mark says. "I don't think it's drugs," he says, and I laugh.

$isi opens her eyes. "What's so fucking funny?"

* * *

When Mark calls me with the news, he sounds shaky. The buzz of my anxiety shoots from the bottom of my throat, and I feel like throwing up in my mouth on hearing his quiet *Howareyou?*

"I'm excellent," I say in an attempt to contaminate him with my positive attitude.

"Are you sitting down?"

"I'm sitting down." I spring up from my couch. I walk over to the window. If the news is really bad, I'll jump. I'm kidding.

"A tumour."

A tumour. It seems impossible. It seems impossible that even a small sick-looking creature like $isi would be capable of housing anything so rotten. "Jesus."

"I'm talking to Jennifer later on. We'll need to figure out a strategy. It's going to get out sooner rather than later. She's going for treatments."

"What kind of tumour? Is it bad?" I say, trying to remember what it was that my grandmother died of. Something humiliating, requiring a catheter and a bag, pelvis bones breaking and her insides just melting into a toxic mass before she passed on.

"It's operable. It's in her brain. It apparently runs in her family."

"We should have genetic testing before we sign them up," I say and then quickly add, "Mark, I'm just kidding. I'm just in shock," before Mark has a chance to say something or, worse, hang up.

"I'm in shock, too. She's a young girl."

"Practically a child," I say. Then I have a brilliant idea. I frequently have brilliant ideas in the morning. "We need to use this," I say.

"Use what?"

"The cancer. It's an opportunity. Cancer kills, I know, but obscurity is a mass killer. We'll send her on a tour – something smaller, you know, more intimate setups – but we'll attach the *tumour* to it all. This could be a Thing. It's better than drugs."

"You are insane."

"No. I'm not. We own it. Flaunt it. They have those ribbons that they wear, right? I think they're different colours for different body parts. So we'll come up with a colour scheme for her. We make a logo or something. Her logo is whatever, brown, the ribbon is brown; it's perfect. Talk to Pig – Jennifer about it."

"I'm hanging up now."

"Before you do, can you imagine the press? She can do inspirational interviews right away. Maybe a blog where she talks about the treatment."

"You want to exploit $isi's tumour."

"Of course. Or no, not exploit it. Give her the voice. You know, inspire people. Other women. Use her celebrity to bring the world's attention to it – how bad can that be? How bad is it anyway?"

"Not sure. She has to have surgery. Then chemo. Maybe. It's mostly preventive from what she tells me, but she's going to be pretty out of service for most of it."

"That's fine. She doesn't even have to pretend to play the guitar anymore, she can just do a little dance or something when they perform. Or talk about the cancer in the intervals. Go sit down somewhere on the stage so that she's visible, so that they can see her and think about it and, you know, feel feelings. They'll buy albums out of guilt if nothing else."

"Christ," Mark says, but his tone of voice has changed. I'm very sensitive to small things like that, tone of voice, eyes. People can tell you their life story by the way they speak, the way they look at you. How they sit, too. Nervous laughter, rapid blinking, fiddling with jewellery.

This is extremely useful when picking up women. Knees away when you sit side by side: she's mad at you. Vulgar jokes: she's desperate, wants you to relax around her.

Anyway, right now, with Mark, his voice, what I notice is that some spark comes back to it. He would hate to admit it, but Mark and I are similar; he is just pretending not to be for his own sake, for *his* peace of mind. How hard it must be living with all these restraints, pretending to be nice.

After our phone call, I pour myself some sparkling water and drop a perfect, clean mint leaf into the glass. I sit in front of a window, letting my eyes lose focus, blurring out the apartments across the street, smudging the crawly little lives inside them.

I picture $isi's future: her big-eyed face, her little cherry mouth that speaks in a wispy voice into a microphone to a sea of her look-alikes, black-and-white-haired girls, choking up at every honest word she says about her struggle, her need to go on, her spirit of survival. It's lovely. She's wearing white. White nail polish. Later we – she talks about the special kind of... *energy* at her shows. The energy. The support of her fans. What keeps her going. The purity. The love.

I call her number but it goes straight to voice mail. I tell her I know. I'm here to help. I mean it.

I order a bouquet of flowers. White roses and, I tell the girl on the phone, whatever other white flowers go with roses so it's not just roses; it has to be unique; it's for a unique person. The girl on the phone giggles because she's an idiot.

13

AS MUCH AS I DON'T WANT TO ADMIT IT, WHAT'S GOING ON with $isi has got to me. What does it say about my judgment, signing up artists who are such liabilities? Addictions, unstable behaviour in general, hysterics? Cancer. I'd blame my inability to foresee, but foresight is nonsense. How could I have known? I couldn't have.

I wake up with those sorts of anxious thoughts. The cleaning lady has done a nice job while I was away in Montreal, but I notice a tiny stain on the flat-screen TV and jump out of bed, irritated, trying to wipe off the stain with a sleeve of my silk pajama top. I succeed; the stain disappears.

I unpack my suitcase; sort out the shirts to take to the dry cleaner.

I get dressed. A crisp white Etro shirt, black raw-Japanese-denim jeans Gloria bought me on sale at Saks last Boxing Day. I don't get things on sale, but Gloria kept insisting, and I remember feeling too tired to argue with her so I let her pick my clothes. The pleasure it gave her to dress me up like I was a baby made up for the spa gift certificate I gave her for Christmas. She had deemed the certificate "so impersonal it is almost insulting."

I think of calling Gloria but I don't want to confide in her. Confiding in her would confuse her – we're already a little too close, and I know she'd be eager to try to comfort me, which would mean I would owe her. I would probably have to book a weekend in the country to pay for showing my vulnerability. And then, who knows? Maybe she'll bring up *combining our lives*, as she has done recently, alarmingly. Instead, I call Jason. He says it's terrible. What happened with $isi.

"It is," I say. "I wonder if our thing released something in her, turned on some kind of a switch in her brain that caused the tumour."

"That's the dumbest thing I've ever heard you say."

"An earthquake in the amygdala."

"So poetic!"

"Thank you." I read the phrase online in an article about brain tumours. It would make a song title, why not?

* * *

I eat very little. Smoothies and delivery from the deli in Whole Foods. I drink water from my new Aquasafe reverse-osmosis filter system I had installed a few days ago. The filter is supposed to remove major water contaminants such as lead or pesticides. I pour a glass of water from the bathroom and I drink to see if I can detect the difference between the old water and the new water. Both old water and new water taste like water. I weigh the glass in my hand and consider throwing it against the wall. I'm not sure why. To experience throwing a glass against the wall? I think about the shards exploding, finding pieces of them weeks afterwards, stepping on them unaware, glass fibres burying into the soles of my feet, the pain.

I set the glass back down on the counter.

I send Dog away to a kennel, pay somebody else to walk and feed him.

I don't work out. I can't concentrate on my workouts, and there's no point in doing them if they're not done as they should be.

Jason calls, but I stop answering my phone.

I don't answer my phone and don't turn on my computer.

I ignore a personal visit from the reps for the video production company behind the new Charlie video. I send them away as soon as they show up on the intercom screen, their eager little eyes staring right into the camera as if they could see right into me looking back at them.

My only contact with the world is via my mail and the mysterious roses that are delivered every second day. I guess someone got the address wrong, but I can't be bothered to check. Just imagining myself on hold with some bitchy customer service rep makes me exhausted.

This has happened before, this sudden, unprovoked agoraphobia. This time it's all her fault. It's all my fault. I wish for the tumour to turn out deadly. Swiftly deadly. To erase her. And with her, erase all the guilt. Because this thing, it's guilt – it's guilt that I'm dealing with, isn't it? So unexpected and violent, slick like an organ falling out of my abdominal cavity, landing on my neon-white floor.

The tumour is not deadly. Too bad.

It's a terrible thing to wish on a young girl, death. There's something wrong with me. Or maybe I'm just better at admitting to what I really feel about life; how human I really am. We're here only for a short time, so why lie? But of course, we need to lie. We lie to survive. We lie even to ourselves.

I am devastated about $isi's tumour.

I walk around. There's lots of room to walk around. My suite is on the top floor, with wraparound windows. I can see into other buildings. People are so indiscreet – flaunting their blurred asses and blurred faces, their silly blurry lives, to the world. I'm reminded of naked mole rats I once saw at a zoo. The rats' cross-sectioned tunnels were visible to the public. The animals, pink and blind, would try to lurch forward, frantically crushing each other inside the plastic sausage – the blades of yellow teeth, gunky paws swiping – unaware of their shame.

A feeling of loneliness comes over me sometimes when I get stuck on a particular window, watching the human mole rats go about their lives – eating dinners, hugging in kitchens, fucking in bedrooms. Bodies pressed against the glass in the more exhibitionistic dwellings; sometimes, in the next room, their ratlings' faces, too, pressed against the glass. I could never be them, hugging in a kitchen, pressing a wife against a glass window, inserting a child into a crib.

The feeling of loneliness vanishes.

To rest from pacing, I lie down on the cool floor and look at the ceiling (steel beams, pipes). The ceilings are high, which gives me the feeling of being free, yet being locked in, stuck in a contained galaxy, a large aquarium. I keep my aquarium as plain as possible. The noise and chaos outside is enough, and even though I can't hear it, I imagine it filtering through every little crack and open window.

For art, I have a couple of framed posters – *Keep Calm and Carry On* covering a safe – and a couple of black-and-white photographs of buildings. I have one large black-and-white photograph of Gloria's back and ass, given to me by Gloria last year on my thirty-first birthday. I don't know what to think of it. I don't look at it much. The most impressive feature in the main space is a mass of wires, glass and metal with seven different kinds of light bulbs that hangs between the kitchen and the pullout. It was made by a designer friend of Gloria's. You can operate the bulbs to dim or, alternatively, shine brightly with a remote control. I enjoy playing with it, changing the moods of my space with the movement of my fingers.

I never cook for anyone here; no one stays here except for me, not even Gloria.

14

OUTSIDE, TORONTO TURNS FROM SEPTEMBER TO EARLY
October and everything is bathed in yellowish-green-soon-
to-be-red-and-brown-and-then-dead hues.

I think about $isi obsessively. Today, I've been thinking
how I met her. She sent a demo of herself singing an Amy
Winehouse song. She was raw and young and strange, but
there was something to her that made me look twice, made
me listen to the demo and then made me replay it twice more.

She was a serious girl in that video, with a pale face and
a big nose and lips that were too big even for the nose. She
wasn't plain. She wasn't like the girls I sleep with. She was
jolie laide – an ugly beauty: a face of too many wrong angles
and a smile that could fix everything in a flash.

She excited me like no one else excited me before – it
wasn't sexual, at least not all of it. It was as if her little video
and her presence in it gave me some kind of elusive peace
of mind that I'm so keen on. I phoned Jason and told him
about it.

"You sound like you're in love," he said.

"I might be. I'm smitten."

"I've never heard you say that before."

"I feel inspired."

"I bet."

"Not like that."

He was wrong. But it didn't matter. I didn't need his feedback. I just wanted to tell someone about her. She was what I'd been looking for, for years, a cookie-cutter sensitive girl who was distinctive enough to possibly make it big.

I called her and flew her in. She showed up with her mother, who was all bleached hair and bad skin, who smoked and said almost nothing the entire time. When she did speak, she spoke softly. She twitched, couldn't wait to leave. She might've been on something. I never asked. She seemed ready to sell her daughter to whoever would buy her. So I bought her.

After her mother left, $isi moved into a place I'd rented for her. In the recording studio, she squealed and jumped and threw her arms around necks by way of greetings. She wrote notes for everyone, thanking them for working with her. She would come by with Tupperware full of cookies and cupcakes that she never touched because she was worried about getting fat.

I hired a stylist to come up with a look for her. I hired someone else to bleach her teeth. I hired a music coach to get her in shape and started making phone calls to all my contacts to get her promoted. Then we gave her a name. She was no longer Sylvia. And once people received her studio-slick demo, they called us right back.

She cried in the cab after not winning anything at her first awards show.

I made some jokes, but I'm not very good with jokes. *Knock knock.*

I tried calling Mark and getting him to come down, but he was away in Europe that week, annoyingly unreachable. By this time, $isi and I were in a booth at a club, with a curtain separating us from the crowd dancing on the floor. I didn't really know what else to offer her. I put my hand on her tiny shaking knee and she looked up at me with teary, mascara-gooped-up eyes and opened her lips a little, enough to see her tongue.

There was a bottle of sparkling wine chilling in a silver bucket. I ordered sparkling despite the fact that there was nothing to celebrate. Or there was, as I kept insisting. It was an honour to just be nominated. So we celebrated.

I spend one more night of moping around in my condo. I listen to music of my late teenage years, when I went through a brief period of dark clothing and makeup, and locking myself in my room even though my parents were nice and I had no reason to lock myself in my room. But I liked to imagine that I had bad parents; a father who shouted outside my door, an absent mother who stumbled around the house all day in an open robe with a cigarette. The music was dark: morbid, heavy beats of electro and synth. It begged my life to be tragic. I'm tragic now; I'm seventeen again, and I am depressed for no good reason. I lie on the floor in the darkness until I fall asleep. No dreams.

* * *

I wake up refreshed, as if after a detox.

I want to go outside.

I'm hungry.

I want to see people.

I want to fuck.

There's only a chunk of stale bread left in the breadbox. I make French toast.

I shower. In the shower, I shout my own name over and over to test the timbre and strength of my voice – it comes out in a croak at first, but then it booms through the apartment, bouncing off the concrete walls, echoing back to me, filling my ears with its strength.

I call Dog's kennel and ask them when I can pick him up. I want some company and Dog's company is the best way to ease into it, a training ground for the company of others.

I collect all of the roses that have been accumulating in the little vestibule by the elevator. It's the same kind of arrangement every time – six deep, bloody red roses with shaved-off thorns, each bunch wrapped with a thick red velvet ribbon. There's a sticker attached to the ribbon with the name of the delivery company and a number.

I call the number to try to find out where the roses are coming from. The robotic-voiced woman won't even tell me if they're an international delivery or not.

Maybe $isi is behind the flowers. I wonder if it's some perverse way of showing that she pines for me, or if it's the result of her being high on medication. If it's a reply to the white roses I sent to her when she was in the hospital for the first time, overnight.

Wherever they're coming from, I throw them all out because they're shedding black flakes all over the floor.

I call Gloria and make a plan to fuck her later. I'll have to go through the usual sequence of dinner, drinks and light-yet-serious relationship talk where she will ask me where we stand, have I found somebody else, and where I will say she has nothing to worry about, I'm all hers, and I love what she's done with her hair and I would love to taste her, it's been so long.

15

MY IDEA FOR MAKING THE TUMOUR $ISI'S THING TURNS OUT
to be brilliant. Post-tumour, there are TV appearances: morning shows, afternoon shows, even a few evening show
appearances. There are a couple of magazine articles. We get
interview requests – too many, so we have to start turning
them down. $isi has been asked to give advice on everything
from how to be at parties to healthy eating to fashion in the
bedroom. For the latest release, we rejig the lyrics so that
the song has the word *grey* in it. The ribbon colour for brain
tumour is grey. With a nod toward Amy Winehouse's "Back
to Black," the writer comes up with a title: "Black to Grey."

Although $isi is on the way to recovery, it's important
to continue with our Thing, to keep giving it a positive
spin. Everyone works hard to keep the tumour issue in the
public eye.

I have many ideas.

I call Piglet. "What about the destigmatizing angle. Let's destigmatize it. We can talk about the stigma. How $isi is trying to do that – how she's not shying away from talking about dark subjects. Like tumours."

"Very good."

"You like it?"

"We just need to come up with a new word. She says she hates saying that word."

"Tumour?"

"It's an ugly word," she says.

"We should have a coffee someday," I say.

"I'm allergic to caffeine."

"Tea then."

"I'll call $isi right now," Jennifer says. "I have to go." She hangs up.

I throw the phone at the couch to satisfy my desire to throw it. I will have to ask Mark if we can get another publicist; one I can actually see in person because this is ridiculous.

* * *

I belong to one of those private clubs with leather chairs in the library, a farm-chic dining room and wide counters for doing lines in the bathrooms. In exchange for high membership fees, I have the privilege of spending thirty dollars on martinis that always get served with microscopic trays of salty almonds and sweaty olives.

Gloria loves these places, so I mostly use it to wine and dine her when she's in town. Her favourite is Bibliothèque, the one I belong to. It's filled with ad guys; PR types looking for junket-loving journalists; junket-loving journalists pairing up with PR types, film guys and young MBAs; old guys with money trying to look like young MBAs; and the old guys' Botoxed au pairs.

Despite the leather chairs, Bibliothèque is flashy and full of aimless pretty girls of all types and leg-length. Most are under thirty, or pretend to be. They are not actually aimless even though they look it. The girls come here because this is the place to find a boyfriend, or at least a friendly sponsor, if he happens to be tied down already (sometimes to a former club member, who was once just like them). The girls present their breasts and shoulders and cheeks and teeth and phones, light bouncing off their jewellery and their eyes, like this is a pageant – and in a way, it is. A big aquarium with tropical fish had been installed on the glass rooftop, and I remarked to Gloria that it's like decorating a baby's room – the aquarium is for the girls.

"Because they like the fish. Because the fish are pretty. So they will bring more girlfriends here to look at the fish."

"So the girls are like the fish?"

"A woman needs a fish like a man needs a bicycle," I laughed.

Gloria didn't laugh. "Are you having a stroke?"

Gloria's company can be exhausting. Some days it's like hanging out with a homeroom teacher. Anyway, the aquarium disappeared one day. A waitress tells me all the fish died after someone threw cocaine in the tank.

I'm immune to the girls in here. Even the plain ones are too much, adorned in their sparkly bits, lines memorized from one of those books about how to catch and train a man. Sometimes when I'm here, I picture myself wrapped inside a giant condom to keep all the mental illness and sparkly filth away.

I would like to stay away from these clubs for good, but right now I need this place in order to find someone to help me to keep the Tumour Thing going. I go to Bibliothèque night after night, pretending to be a bland-yet-exuding-friendliness type – a guy everyone wants to talk to because you can just tell he will listen.

I'm an okay actor, save for the inability to tell jokes. I can become a friendly person, a chatting/listening machine, asking about people's jobs, their clothes and the television they like. People love talking about TV shows. I talk about *The Sopranos*, the greatest TV show that's ever existed. I've never seen it. But almost everyone can and will talk about *The Sopranos*, and no one really listens to anyone, so it doesn't matter that I haven't seen it.

For my outings, I wear a white T-shirt, a black Varvatos suit jacket, a rotation of skinny Tiger of Sweden jeans, always paired with a set of ugly Coach tennis shoes. This outfit makes me look like one of those ad agency guys, exactly who I'm trying to attract.

I sit and wait. I check my Facebook. Try to come up with clever status updates. I scroll through the recipes I've posted. I count my comments. Not a lot of comments. I message my new Mexican clicker to request more comments.

I look up from Facebook to look at people. I shouldn't look too busy. I should look inviting.

A girl journalist starts chatting with me. *The Sopranos* comes up. She tells me she's just like Adriana. I have no idea what that means, but she seems proud of herself, so I say, "Interesting," and she smiles and squints at me. "What do you do?"

I could probably fuck her, but I won't. "Nothing. Unemployed."

She gasps. She checks her phone. "I have to go."

"Yes, please go," I say, and her eyes turn big and her ponytail whips around and she clicks off on her silver heels.

An older woman with a baby-rat face and a cloud of teased yellow-red hair, wearing black-patent Louboutins that she shows while crossing and uncrossing her legs, has been watching me. She's someone I actually hooked up with once, after Gloria and I had a fight in here and I was left alone to feel bad and remorseful.

"That's Mildred," someone says beside me. "She used to be married to some famous Canadian musician or an actor. She's okay for fifty."

"You should go for it."

"She's a Six," the guy says. I like him.

"A solid Six."

"I don't go anywhere below Seven," he laughs.

"I like anything from One up," I laugh.

He quickly looks behind me. "Yeah? You should go for it yourself then."

"Are you with an ad agency?"

"Who isn't?"

"Anything I'd know?"

"We did that cat food ad. We do a ton of shit, but everyone always talks about the cat food."

"Where you've got guys pretending to be cats? Those were great."

He nods and looks in the direction of the glass door leading to the patio, as if he saw someone there he knows.

I look in the same direction, but there isn't anybody there; he's just one of those guys who is always looking for a better party than the one he's at.

I try to guess his age. Close to mine. But balding. Expensive glasses. I'd ask him where he got the frames but I don't. We'll exchange fashion tips another time.

I say, "I'm in the music business. I need an ad for cancer."

"Like the *Run for the Cure* stuff?"

"Like that, but different. I want to make cancer cool."

"Twisted. I like it." I really do like him.

"Good. I know someone who has a tumour, one of my clients, a pop star. I want people to respond to it positively, you know, connect with it. They have grey ribbons. It's a brain tumour."

"Terrible."

"Yeah. Terrible. But that's my point – we're demonizing it. And it's just part of life. I want to make it acceptable. No drama."

"Drama is bad."

"Unless it's the mentally ill or children. Or seniors."

"Soldiers."

"Yes. Exactly," I say and watch him chug his beer, something behind his eyes whirring, some kind of machine that probably has access to everything that's ever been trendy, trying to come up with the perfect formula for me.

This is why this unpleasant place is okay after all – watching this guy, I become aware of how everyone here is actually working on something. Sure, it's mostly about hookups, about sad lost Sixes like Mildred, but it's also about being on, being ready to talk about making tumours acceptable if it may mean more money, a step up to glory. I'm always impressed with people trying to make something out of themselves.

"Mmm," my new best friend says and takes a sip out of his new bottle of Heineken, which shows up along with my Scotch. Dalwhinnie.

"It should be a WTF strategy," my new best friend says.

"What?"

"The Tumour Thing. You know, WTF, what the fuck, as in, *what the fuck was that?* It's basically a hidden ad, like a teaser. I mean, I don't know what that would be *exactly* right now, but I think that's the route to go."

"We don't tell people it's about a tumour?"

"Precisely. Right. We just do some other stuff, you know, not even related, and then there could be a big reveal. Or not. No drama."

"No. No IVs. Something quiet and sexy instead," I say.

He blinks at me, smiles. "Yeah." Then his eyes lose their focus and he's looking past me. "Ah screw it. She's almost a Six-and-a-half. One more beer and she'll be a Seven."

I recall the feeling of Mildred's teeth on my skin. I look around the rooftop patio. There are transactions buzzing all around me, the eager eyes and mouths, the shiny hair and skin. Everywhere, the ringed fingers and bracelets touching shoulders, shoulders shaking in laughter and iPhones flashing, the tiny trays of olives and almonds everywhere.

I notice two women at a table near us. They are sitting head to head, whispering to each other, hands covering mouths. They're both attractive, with big bodies full of angles, wide faces and slightly upturned eyes. They look Russian. I like how they talk, how absorbed they seem in each other.

I catch a few women who might be glancing toward their table, though I can't be sure because they could be trying to look at me. But not likely – it's the girls, not me, they're interested in. I know enough about the female psyche to know that the girls' giggly familiarity would feel threatening to other women, driving them a little crazy about not being let in on the secret.

I tap the ad guy on the shoulder to ask him what he thinks. "Nine-and-a-half. Both of them. So that's what?"

"Nineteen."

"Nineteen," he giggles. "Listen, my standards are dropping proportionally to time going by. By last call, Mildred will be an Eight." He winks at me. He gets up. He hands me his card. *PAT* on one side, *TRICK@kolektiv* on the other. Thick cardboard paper.

After PAT TRICK leaves, I watch the Nineteens for a short while. I picture them on film, talking about something to do with $isi's situation, giggling and being intimate and best-friendly with each other. There's a rush of sudden happiness, a spark going off in my brain.

* * *

At home, there's a surprise waiting for me. A new bouquet of roses. I put this one in water, intending to give it to Gloria tomorrow when I see her for dinner at Bibliothèque.

16

I MEET PATRICK AT HIS AGENCY. IT'S A WHITE OFFICE, SLICK like a laptop, on the main floor, with the word *Kolektiv* printed in red on the white wall behind a symmetrical, straight-haired secretary, a Seven.

Patrick manoeuvres me through a bright hallway filled with cubicles filled with guys and girls typing on their Macs, toys and boxes of crap towering on their ergonomic desks. The ceiling is punctuated with skylights. Nobody looks up as we walk by. I let out a silent fart.

We go inside a small conference room, where Patrick gestures toward a chair and I sit down across the table from him. He says, "Got your message. We use two girls. Tens. We shave their heads and we shoot them just talking. Just talking to the camera, recording one of those vlogs, yapping on about, I don't know, *The Sopranos*. Or something lighter. Maybe makeup or dating. Or sex. One of them is wearing a ribbon."

"WTF," I say.

"WTF. We'll get someone good to do the script, a funny guy. We've got guys to figure out that kind of thing. It has to be about the feeling of it, right? And the look, too."

I say, "Young, but a bit weary around the eyes. Russians or something. We get them to be rude and sexy and bald and hot and the ribbon is there, maybe just one of them is wearing it. I'll hire someone good to write a bitchy opinion piece in *Slate* or *Salon*."

"Bald?"

"Chemo."

"Right. Yeah, man. And we play your client's music in the background, then louder, maybe third episode or something, and it'll be totally accidental, just some quiet song or something in the beginning," he says. He's wearing an Adidas jacket and a shirt with a video game character on it. Since he's losing his hair already, the effect is that of an aged toddler. I smile encouragingly at him.

"Yeah, so they talk about neutral topics – fashion, shopping, douching, stuff like that. No cancer. At first." Patrick sits up, elbows on the table, fingers massaging temples. He talks fast. "Then we do a second campaign after our numbers go up, but it may just happen naturally, you know people googling the song, and the name of the chick and then cancer, and then we can address it directly. Then if our numbers are good – no, they *will* be good."

I keep smiling at him. He smiles back.

He says, "That tie is great, by the way," as if we were two girlfriends catching up over lunch.

"Thank you. I like your glasses."

"They're Japanese."

"Handcrafted?"

"I guess," he says, and turns the screen of his computer around so that I can read the notes as we talk some more about details: the number of people we need, dates, clothes, etcetera.

I'm finally able to make out the label on his glasses. Charmant.

Eventually, we're done talking about the strategy and he walks me out. He tells me about how Mildred got indignant because he didn't ask her to sleep over. He talks about her tits, which are droopy from what I recall, and he says something about how it's unsettling to see older women shaved – he makes a joke about the skin of plucked chickens. I count down from twenty, and then it's time to shake his hand and I'm out, stepping right into a busy, sunny day in the city.

17

THE PHONE RINGING JERKS ME AWAKE. I'VE FALLEN ASLEEP, deeply and dreamlessly, like a teenager, after yet another whole afternoon of Skypeing with Kolektiv, followed by reading scripts and looking at videos of all of our vlogging candidates. I can't tell the bald, Slavic-featured actresses apart anymore.

The shooting starts next week, and it couldn't be soon enough. $isi's new song, "Black to Grey," is leaking everywhere, showing up on top spots in charts, in celebrity news, in music blogs, new fan pages set up by her teenage fans and their mothers.

I pick up the phone, and the phone says, "Guy, I'm sorry."

"Who is this?" I ask, trying to guess the familiar voice but unable to place it.

"The number you gave me was wrong, but I called your agency and told them I was a cleaning lady at the beach house and there was an emergency," she giggles. "I'm sorry."

"Who is this?"

"Dolores."

She appears then, the way I'd left her in her jean shorts wrapped tightly around her bum, her trusting face.

"Dolores!"

"It's me! I'm sorry! I didn't know how else to get a hold of you. I've got your address, too. I'll visit as soon as I–"

"What is this about, Dolores?"

"What do you mean?"

"Why do you want to visit? Why are you calling me? What's going on with you?" I say, but I already know.

Of course I know. Dolores thinks she is in love and she wants to prove her love by stalking me. She wants to show up on my doorstep with her little suitcase, and she wants to have a romance. She doesn't understand the gap between us. She thinks she has a right to me. She thinks that I am, indeed, a vampire prince who has found her at last, his princess. She thinks that there's actually an *us*.

"Well. I love you," she says simply. As if that answered all my questions.

"Dolores–"

"I know, I know, it's crazy, and I was even thinking that you gave me the wrong number on purpose and you haven't been answering my emails? But then I thought you couldn't do that, not you, I mean, we connected, no? Like, we really connected. I looked at the paper and it was clear that the one was really a seven and that I was just an idiot for misreading it. But now here I am. So I was thinking of booking the ticket–"

"No. But I'd love to have a coffee or something if you're ever in town," I say. Coffee. Not risky; things come up at the last minute; everyone cancels coffees all the time. It's almost expected.

"What?"

"When you're in town. We'll have coffee. Right now is not the best time," I say.

"Oh. So you really don't want to see me?" Her voice is small. I see her eyes then, opened wide, the whites so white, the blues so blue.

"It's not that, it's—"

It's exactly that. Why won't I just say it? I won't just say it because I am not a dick. Women love me. And because of that, sometimes, I need to lie and present myself in the best possible light, and simply telling her to fuck off is not something I can stand behind a hundred percent just yet.

I know, I know, for all the $isi lessons, I'm still lacking the ability to make myself absolutely clear. I'm trying to quickly come up with something to end this conversation without hanging up abruptly and calling my phone provider to give me a new number.

"Oh, that's a relief! I couldn't come right away, so I just sent the roses to your address."

"I moved. No roses, Dolores. They probably went to the wrong address," I say. This is a poor strategy. Now I'm going to make her think that I've been sitting here, waiting for something like roses, that I feel wronged by not receiving the roses that she just said she'd been sending.

"So where do you stay now? Different place? I'm trying to book the flight after my mid-terms and it's around Thanksgiving so it's, like, really expensive."

"I'm away during Thanksgiving."

"This is why I'm calling," she says, as if we've had a bunch of conversations already, trying to make plans to meet.

"I'm away the rest of October and November, actually," I say, and there's finally some silence on the other end.

"I can come down sooner?"

"I—"

She says, "Friday? This Friday?"

I look out the window. I scan the building, a grid of glass. I focus on one particular apartment. A man is standing in the window, hand to his ear, shaking his head.

I shake my head, "Listen. I'm going to be honest. I don't want you to come down. I have to go now. I have to take Dog out for a walk."

"What do you mean?"

"That's what I mean, Princess. I don't want you to come down to visit me."

"But, Guy—"

"No. I'm talking now. It's over. We're over. I've met someone else. Her name is Gloria. And I'm sorry. I'm very sorry."

"No."

"No?"

"No. I don't buy it," Dolores says.

My seduction has freed something in her, something much larger than just a glimpse of hope. Faith. A monster of faith – faith so grotesquely enlarged, so clearly and definitely in disproportion to what she realistically should believe about herself. I hang up. I'm a dick.

As soon as I hang up, I block her number.

I pace around my apartment. The dog picks up my nervous energy; he erupts and stops in half-barks as he clicks in circles around the kitchen. When I look at him, he freezes. He looks up from underneath his shy brows. "No kennel. Don't worry."

I almost never talk to Dog, and he looks at me even more stunned when I do. "No kennel," I say. "What?"

Dog keeps staring, his tail slapping the floor unsurely. God, that face. I laugh as he continues staring. Laughing releases the tension that's wound up like a coil around my throat.

I phone Gloria and we make plans to meet at Bibliothèque the next evening.

18

GLORIA SHOWS UP AT BIBLIOTHÈQUE WITH HER NEW ASSIST-
ant. Gloria is a human origami in her white panelled dress.

I introduce everyone, Patrick to Gloria and the new
assistant, Trish, who is very blond and not pretty but not
plain either. A Five. "My friend said they had this awesome
fish tank here," she says, looking around.

"Not anymore," I say like I'm sad.

"Kerry is an account manager now," Gloria explains
when I don't ask what happened to her original assistant.

Patrick talks fast like he's on cocaine. Maybe he's on
cocaine. He is here to show us the first vlog on his iPad – the
just-released vlog that's already got more than ten thousand
views, though Patrick says that more than half of these are
buy-ins. That means they are subscribers to the newsletters
from other products' websites that Kolektiv has worked on.

"Is that legal? To buy out subscriber lists?" Trish, the new
assistant, says. No one answers. She pulls her hair out of a

ponytail and then immediately puts it back into a ponytail. No roots showing. She's probably blond all over.

Patrick opens the first video. On the shiny little screen, two girls with shaved heads sit wide shoulder to wide shoulder. They're both wearing too-big grey T-shirts with low cut-out necks – plain, but looking hot on them. The girl on the right has a tiny grey ribbon pinned to her shirt. They have little or no makeup; I can't decipher. They giggle, touch, whisper and laugh with toothy, wide-open mouths, long necks stretched out.

Their banter is funny, not too scripted, and you can tell that they remember only some of the lines because the conversation veers in unexpected directions. Or perhaps Kolektiv are such geniuses that they make it seem completely unscripted. Either way, it looks authentic, intriguing: Who are these girls and why are they doing this?

The topic of the conversation is guys wearing flip-flops in the city. It seems to be an issue with them, guys and flip-flops and how gross it is.

Throughout the video there's a song playing in the distance, very faintly but, to me, instantly recognizable: $isi's new song. It has a great beat to it, a slightly dreamy synthesizer sequence that makes one think of an enchanted forest, at least according to the producer's note. The song comes on after some distant radio static. It's as if there was something else going on in another room and the song just happens to be playing at the moment. The video ends with the girl on the right, the one with the ribbon, moving toward the screen, turning off the camera.

"Who are they?" Trish says. She's got teeth like a bunch of piano keys squeezed into a small box.

Gloria is staring at me. I smile at Gloria. No one answers Trish. Patrick stares at Gloria. He leans back in his chair like he's cool.

I have no way of telling whether Gloria liked the vlog or not, but her eyes are sharp. They go all cloudy if stuff bores her. I want Gloria's company to take on the Tumour Thing since Piglet doesn't seem to be working out.

"I love it," Gloria says, and Patrick's relaxed pose relaxes even more.

"I don't know, guys. I don't get it," Trish says, and all three of us turn to look at her.

"But do you like it?" Patrick says.

"I don't know. Yes."

Gloria says in a gentle voice, "Would you watch them again?"

Out of the corner of my eye, I see Mildred at the bar, talking to a man who is ignoring her. She leans into him, her frizzy head touching his shoulder, but he just sits there, unmoving, like a stand-in for a man, lifeless. I touch my ear, close my eyes briefly to recall her – her teeth clamping onto my earlobe.

"You okay, honey?" Gloria says. "You're making faces."

"I'm fine. So, would you watch the vlogs," I say, looking at Trish.

"Yeah, for sure. I guess there's something about it."

"You don't know what it is, but you like it," Patrick says.

"Yeah. I think?"

Gloria's smile is tight. I grab her hand under the table and squeeze it quickly. I've never done such a thing. She blinks a few times, hard. I look forward to unzipping her dress later, peeling her out of its white panels, running my hands over her muscled, slim body. I can almost taste the saltiness that isn't there, is never there. Which is, I suppose, why I desire her as strongly as I do – for the saltiness that is never there but should be there. The promise of it, or perhaps the disillusionment when I miss it.

"Excellent," Patrick says and looks at his watch.

After Patrick leaves, we order a tray of finger foods. Root vegetable chips, prosciutto-wrapped breadsticks with fig dip and asiago slivers with a tray of Gaeta olives.

Trish pops an olive into her shiny pink mouth. She sees me watching and blushes, looks down. The waiter comes back, refills Trish's glass of white, brings some Perrier for me and a martini for Gloria.

"I thought that was so interesting," Gloria says, and Trish nods, taking a big gulp of her wine.

"It was," I say. I remember the flip-flops and bring them up.

"Oh, women hate them. But it's also because of that article in *GQ*," Gloria says. "It was somebody's manifesto, about how we need to get rid of all the flip-flops in order to improve the economy and just generally raise standards. It was about our standards. About our standards being low and about us having low expectations and not buying good products and good products not being produced. Everybody just wearing one-dollar Chinaswag that make your feet dirty and disgusting, especially in the city."

"So the girls were talking about that too?" Trish says. There's something wrong with her shirt, I notice now. It has a little stain on it, pale brown. It's between her breasts. I imagine her pinching herself there, a drop of blood staining the shirt before she noticed.

Gloria says, "Yes."

I say, "Did you notice the grey ribbon?"

"For sure. I was totally gonna ask him about that," Trish says.

"It's part of the cancer – The Grey Campaign."

"Oh, that makes sense, cool," Trish says. I look at the stain on her shirt again. Force myself to look away.

Gloria says, "So I'll see you tomorrow?"

Trish's eyes go wide; she smiles brightly, "For sure." She grabs her iPad and inserts it into a pink Hello Kitty case. Her purse is pink snakeskin. "It was so nice to meet you," she says to me. Those cute fucked-up teeth sparkle in the dimmed light. Our eyes meet. I would tell her to leave her cheap little pink bra on, but I would ask her to pull her small tits out of it. With the underwire supporting them, they'd point right at me. One nipple would be slightly bigger than the other. There would be a red mark between the tits, the spot that drew blood. She'd scratch at it with her fingernail, without thinking. It would turn out she'd forgotten to shave. She would be obscenely blond between her legs.

"Thank you, honey." Gloria stands up and hugs Trish briefly. Trish breaks the hug first. She clicks away, her ass jiggling left to right. Big ass but small tits.

Gloria doesn't say anything for a while. I get distracted by Mildred at the bar again. She is now even more intimately wrapped around the unmoving shoulders next to her.

"Oh, Guy," Gloria says.

"What?"

"Seriously," she laughs. "That bitch is old. And Trish is a baby."

"I wasn't—"

She laughs harder. I join in, laugh with her and think about Trish's stained top, the teeth, the way she wobbled away on her high heels. I pull Gloria close, her body hot with remains of laughter. My fantasy Trish bouncing up and down, up and down. Mildred biting my ear. It was strange, teenage-like, her teeth on my ear. She said she loved my energy. Her son was only ten years younger than me, she said. I said I didn't believe it. I told her if I could I would put her ass in a frame and hang it on the wall in my office. That's what you say to women her age. They like hearing that their asses are worth hanging on walls in frames. It makes them feel like they are better than the women my age, women much younger than they are. They like hearing, too, that they couldn't possibly be mothers, not with those asses.

I pull Gloria's face close to mine and I kiss her. "Let's get out of here," I say after her tongue leaves my mouth. I need a body to relieve myself into.

19

I'M NOT A FAN OF AWARD CEREMONIES. TOO LOUD. TOO many peasants. Your face hurts from smiling – cameras flashing and people screaming at you, and you always end up looking like a lonely tampon against all those red backdrops. But it's good for me to go out to these things occasionally, to make nice with people from the industry.

Gloria is excited because she rarely goes to parties where she doesn't have to promote something.

Tonight, she's wearing a powder-blue dress with a cinched waist and a full skirt, very 1950s. It's unusual for Gloria, who prefers simple, straight-line clothing. She does her hair in a sort of layered bun; it looks very nice. I'm proud of her looking so glamorous.

I match her in my charcoal Tiger of Sweden suit, a purple-almost-black Paul Smith tie and white Thomas Pink shirt. I'm wearing handmade John Lobb shoes, which are the biggest fashion extravagance I've ever allowed myself.

I've hired a consultant on a few occasions and we've gone shopping together. Henri. We've had many intimate moments: Henri adjusting my shoulders, straightening my trousers, running his hand over my butt. Henri with his arms folded, an eyebrow cocked. Henri with his hand to his mouth. Henri watching me emerge from the vaginal folds of heavy curtains in the change room at Bloomingdales, strutting around in my winter charcoal greys, my summer light greys, my wild-card shiny stripes. All for him. Then, later on, the two of us arguing playfully over the width of tie, the shade of pink. Henri holding my foot briefly before passing it to the shoemaker, who took measure of my feet. "You have such high arches," Henri said, dreamily, once.

* * *

Before the awards, I sit on Gloria's balcony and drink my sparkling wine. I move my toes in my shoes, which hold them tightly, lovingly, as if they were Henri's hands.

Gloria's apartment, similarly to mine, overlooks a cluster of towers with mole rats in every single available compartment.

She joins me and we click our glasses, a gentle click like a nod. "I'm sorry about the other day," she says.

I don't know what she's talking about. There's nothing to be sorry for, I want to tell her, but maybe there is something to be sorry for.

"I'll be thirty-nine next month," she says.

"Yes," I say, even though her math is off.

"It's crazy, no?" she says. "It feels like I'm running out of time."

"Running out of time? We're all running out of time. What's crazy?" I know what's crazy. Maybe that's what she's sorry for. Children. Talking about children. She's been bringing up children, hinting at children. Perhaps she should adopt, after all. I try to recall the conversation we had with Jason in the summer. Gloria adopting a child to provide inspiration for a book she wanted to write? I can't recall the details.

"I didn't mean to get all serious," she says, which only makes this more serious. I wish we could just call a car now and get to the awards. But there's still a bit of time to kill.

I think about my mother and father; my mother and father having their little fights right before they'd be due to go somewhere, where they'd have to pretend that nothing had happened. Hating each other politely the whole evening. At parties, they were probably surrounded by others who had committed similar offences before going out, all of them in the same room. Rooms full of offenders and the offended.

"Anyway. I think it would be great if $isi won, don't you?"

"She's okay."

"You can be such a dick," Gloria says, affectionately, but there's a tiny tremble in her voice, which tells me that she means it, too. I let it go. I'm not going to have a fight. Tonight is going to be good. There will be no fights tonight.

We stay on the balcony for a dull eternity, and she talks about TV shows and books and clothes and other things, and I say *hmm* and *right* and *I know*, and then it's time to call the car.

* * *

At the awards, we're seated near the stage. There are many painfully scripted introductions and even more painful performances. $isi doesn't win for best song or best video, which draws some boos from the back of the room. There are hordes of teenagers with hand-drawn posters – *$isi, we love you!* and *Black to Grey!* – in the back of the room.

Gloria, next to me, is mostly silent throughout the evening, save for some words of encouragement when $isi's name is read out for the third time. And for the third time, $isi doesn't win.

It's a good thing she's not attending the event. According to Mark, she's in Europe with her mother, relaxing in an infinity pool in Spain.

I picture her mother sitting angrily in the shade, smoking cigarettes and watching the new-and-improved $isi swimming laps, her bald head bobbing above the water like a pool toy.

Near the end of the awards, there's a dull segment honouring Fatima, the recently deceased musician who often took breaks from her career due to exhaustion. Then the awards are over.

* * *

Coming out of the theatre, there's a riot of camera lights. Flash. Flash. Flash. Demands to pose this way or that.

I have no "bad side." I'm okay with the cameras showing up wherever they happen to be, but Gloria, the former model, keeps manoeuvring me around, trying to expose her right half-profile to all the flashes.

There are people screaming everywhere. Mostly they just scream the names of all the stars that come out of the building, but there are a few screams shouting my name as well. I don't know how kids find out these things, but they do.

Despite all this chaos, I isolate an especially frantic movement to my right, out of the corner of my eye. Somebody is running in my direction.

I hear my name – *Guy, Guy, Guy* – and I let go of Gloria. Next, a body is throwing herself at me, face covered with hair. I can't get a good look. I stand there as she lands on me heavily, like a mattress. I sway but don't fall.

I see a massive guy in black running toward us, shouting into his headset. The crowds are screaming behind the red line. A couple more people seem to be breaking through, running. More guys in black start showing up, running after them.

The woman has wrapped her arms around me. I can smell her – her smell is familiar. And then her body, her body, too, feels familiar, although it seems bigger now, more dangerous.

I can hear Gloria shouting something, to me or to the security guy who starts peeling Dolores off me. Dolores is holding onto my neck. It's very unpleasant, all this tugging and moving. Now, I'm pushing her off, too. She only clings harder. Her strength seems to have doubled from the resistance. Another guy in black runs up and tries to help peel her off. Finally, she falls through their hands to the ground, where she crashes, a sack filled with hefty bones.

At this point Gloria is pulling me away, back to the exit where they're ushering all of the people who are still on the red carpet.

I look at where Dolores was lying on the ground, except she's not on the ground anymore. She's running toward one of the scaffolding towers holding the enormous spotlights that shine onto the carpet. She starts scaling the scaffolding fast, like an enormous ape.

People are shouting even more, now. There are more men in black with headsets. The entire red carpet seems to be filled with them. Someone is urging us to keep moving, keep moving, but I want to see. I stand in one spot, not moving, no one paying attention to me at all, except Gloria, who is pulling on my arm.

She stops pulling on my arm. We stand still. We are watching Dolores climb higher, at last stopping about twelve feet above the ground.

The crowd is taking pictures, shouting at her, shouting at the guys in black, just shouting anything they can think to shout: *Get down, come down, get down, get her... blah blah blah.*

I should maybe talk to Patrick about this, see if Kolektiv could stage something like this with our tumour campaign. Some kind of an event where one of the bald models could do a drastic public stunt. I don't know what exactly – a similar scaffold climb?

I watch Dolores, with her wild hair and a blouse that seems to have ripped slightly on the side, revealing a stack of two soft, fleshy folds – she's gotten a little larger since the summer – and I feel excited, even turned on.

Gloria's talking but it's all just noise; I'm too distracted to listen. An absurd thought, perhaps from shock: *My girl. That's my girl.*

"Oh my god, I think she's trying to jump," Gloria's faint voice suddenly forms itself into a coherent whole in my head. Once she says that, I know she's right. And I also know that I have to do something about that. It's in my best interest, as there might be some kind of a consequence, maybe already is, something like a blog post somewhere, some kind of lunatic tragic-romantic rant posted on Facebook.

The guys in black are talking to Dolores, telling her to get down. The lights at the top of the scaffold get turned off so the tower is dark, but the other lights illuminate her still. An ambulance arrives along with a fire truck amidst a blast of sirens. A police car, then another one, lights flashing everywhere. The street becomes a techno show.

Please.

She's not climbing any higher, but she's not climbing down either. I could ask her to come down. She would listen to me. *Please come down, Princess.*

I think of all the future talks I may have to have with Gloria and possibly the police and maybe even the press – how bothersome it will all be – but I know it's going to be better than Dolores climbing to the top, jumping off and possibly leaving incriminating proof of our connection with each other.

"Dolores, please come down," I say as loudly as I can. I can't see her face well, can't see her eyes at all, but I know she is watching me. The noise around us seems to quiet down, or I tune it out. All I hear is some soft whimpers from above.

"Come on, sweetie," I shout, and don't even choke over the *sweetie*, which is not a word I use. I can't say *princess* out loud, not in front of Gloria.

Dolores looks down. We lock eyes. *Come on, Princess,* I mouth. She nods once. Then she's moving. She takes the first hesitant step, her foot landing on the nearest metal rod below her.

Gloria squeezes my arm. She asks me something about Dolores: *Is she a friend? How do I know her?*

I watch Dolores. A few feet above the ground, she loses her footing and tumbles down, heavily, ungracefully; there is a funny noise as she lands. I am close enough now to hear it, and I notice her face, those round eyes full of surprise.

The paramedics and the firefighters rush to her side, there's more shouting, the men in black are running, someone pushes me away.

* * *

Three hours later, we're at the hospital in the waiting room. It was Gloria's idea to come here, and I don't know why I agreed, but I did. We could've just gone home. But Gloria insisted that it was our obligation to at least show up at the hospital until someone from Dolores' family could come. The family is miles and hours away and the earliest anyone can come is tomorrow afternoon. I don't plan on sitting here until tomorrow afternoon, and I certainly don't plan to talk to Dolores when she wakes up, but I sit here because Gloria has asked me to.

There's a social worker coming to see Dolores when she wakes up, and there are two police officers sitting in the waiting room with us. They leave us alone, though I have to give them a call later, I am told, which is fine with me.

* * *

I fall in and out of nervous bleeps of sleep lasting a second or two; eventually, I give up and force myself to watch a short segment on home renovations on the TV.

I don't know how long Gloria wants to sit here and wait. The update is that Dolores knocked herself unconscious when she fell, and they're monitoring her for signs of concussion. She has also broken an ankle. She's not unconscious right now, but is sleeping thanks to a sedative they've given her. I wish they'd give me a sedative.

"Isn't it funny?" Gloria says when she sees me awake.

"What's funny?"

"Well, I just think how this is funny, how it feels like we're sitting here like we're her parents or something."

"Parents. I'm exhausted."

"I know. I really feel for her," she says.

"Well, yes, she is very disturbed. But that has nothing to do with us. She's just one of those mentally ill superfans. Anything to get to $isi. It's scary, but it's not uncommon."

"I feel responsible. We saw her climb that tower, we *witnessed* it."

"The police seem to be okay with us leaving."

"I know. But we're connected by that experience, all of us."

"Maybe you could adopt her."

"Very funny," Gloria says. She looks at me like she is sad. She may be sad.

"I'm sorry."

She closes her eyes and slumps in her chair. Her party dress is a bit filthy, dust and grease, as if it was she who'd been climbing on things. Her updo is in place, but it seems like a wig now in its perfect form that clashes with the rest of her. In the hospital light, her skin has a pale green shade to it, the powder, or whatever makeup stuff she's wearing on her face, visible in tiny, uniform specks, some of it more concentrated in the skin's ridges where the wrinkles are.

I enjoy seeing her so unguarded and imperfect.

An older woman can be as fascinating as a younger one. But some have been too dulled by disappointment, by the resentment of having youthful dreams disappear, and then later on, that disappointment hardens like a scar. The skin is thinner and everything hurts: getting passed over for promotion, watching her best friend get married to her crush, or getting married and watching her husband stroke the remote control with more fondness than he'd have for her breast. And then even later, troubled children, divorces, funerals. Other ex-wives at funerals; what to wear to funerals with other ex-wives present.

I can't really offer an older woman anything in terms of experience; there isn't a lot I can open her to. I can give her a lightning of romance, a wild weekend in the country where we explore her unloved vagina and talk about her failed relationship with the last married man she met at her work Christmas party, but that's about it.

I think about Mildred. How she wrapped herself around the unmoving shoulders of the man at the club. How it made me tired just watching this.

But Gloria is relatively untouched, not bitter, and perhaps this is what attracts me to her – that I can still find a certain innocence to her, that her eyes still widen; the world still surprises her. She was a princess, she had princes, she was on the cover of a magazine – all of her dreams came true.

She's like a girl who seems overgrown, a girl who seems to have aged by accident, who has found herself in this older woman's body one Alice-in-Wonderland morning.

I appreciate Gloria. And now, in this washed-out green hospital hallway at three a.m., I feel that there's nothing wrong with trying to have her in my life a little more – there will be no unpredictability of the sort I've had with $isi and Dolores. There's safety, a notion that I've landed somewhere dull but beautiful: a five-star resort in a politically unchallenged country.

And I need a vacation.

I take her hand in mine and give it a quick squeeze and let go. She leans into me, rests her face on my shoulder. Her tiredness spills all over me, and I pull her close, drape my arm around her wide shoulders. And then these words come out of my mouth: "Let's just go. Let's go to my place."

She stirs and sits up, looks up at me, her eyes scanning my face, and I close my eyes once to affirm, show her that I mean it, that I really want her to come over to my place, stay the night, god, maybe even stay a couple of nights, stay many nights if that's what it'll take to get her out of here and if that's what it'll take for me to get some peace of mind.

PART II

Why is it a surprise to find that people other than ourselves are able to tell lies?
– Alice Munro, "The Spanish Lady"

20

I SURVIVE THE SPRING AND SUMMER AND FINALLY GET TO
the end of it.

There isn't a lot to tell – or there is. Gloria and I become
exclusive at her insistence. This, ultimately, means that we
somehow own each other – each other's genitals and actions
and possibly even thoughts.

In my adult life, I have never had a long-term exclusive
relationship like this, so I am not entirely sure what to expect.
There is some residual part of me, a ghost of my childhood
naïveté, that keeps insisting this kind of arrangement is for
something – that there is a huge prize at the end of it all, an
endurance prize, a Lifetime Achievement Award – but this
idea is absurd. If I were to use one of Gloria's adages: it just
doesn't feel like me. I only go along with it because I have
no mind or energy to argue it. I have reserves of it, energy,
that I need for my work, and my mind is anaesthetized by
the predictability that a serious – what a romantic word
that is, *serious* – relationship brings.

Being with Gloria is similar to the time in college when I swore off sleeping with women, except that I am sleeping with a woman – I'm majoring in one woman. Whatever I'm doing with my major should count as some kind of home-work – the routine of intimate dinners, the long walks with Dog, the cinema on Fridays, the small cocktail parties for PR friends, the grocery shopping trips that are only slightly less interesting than cocktail parties.

The sex. How quickly the regular sex is dismissed, then taken up to another level because of Gloria's initiative to keep me happy.

I don't have a problem with kinky, but what we do doesn't seem organic, there's no spontaneity – it is forced, like a list of activities that we must get through – homework, again, or a prescription from a chick mag, a check mark beside each item:

- The Magic Fingertip Trick
- The Start-Stop-Start Technique
- A Wild New Use for Your Loofah
- Foreplay Men Crave: Touch His Secret Erotic Spot (Surprise: It Doesn't Rhyme with *Shmenis*).

I am passive – not in bed, but in going along with the list, in letting *Cosmopolitan* and dildos direct my life. The wooden Dalmarko trunk that Gloria buys at a designer showroom sale accumulates a variety of rubber, silicone, plastic, leather and combo-material sex toys that we use dutifully on each other, short-circuiting each other's genitals till orgasm. We spend months rubbing and prodding, tugging and kneading and clamping.

There are a few weeks when there is none of that stuff at all – no sex – as Gloria goes through different product launches, festival preparations. One time, when she leaves for a week, I take her torture trunk and shove it deep inside my walk-in closet, then I change my mind and drive the whole shebang to a dump and leave it there.

When she comes back, I tell her about the trunk. She shouts at me, but then I suggest we experiment with her ass – the place that she had never used sexually – which makes her forget about being angry, and about the trunk. After weeks of lube and butt plugs and anal beads and, finally, intercourse, ass fun also manages to turn dull and repetitive.

* * *

The Tumour vlog series is becoming more and more popular, raking in hundreds of thousands of viewers. People finally figure out the answer to the WTF strategy, and when it's discovered that it was a tumour that drove the whole enterprise, we get exposure that doubles and triples the currency of $isi's fame. From hundreds of thousands of viewers, we go to millions. There are articles being written about the tumour and $isi and the vlogs; there are essays in *Personality* magazine, and *Salon* is talking about the idea of making a chronic illness cool: *It's a part of human experience!*

There are photo spreads where the models' heads are shaved, where they look straight into cameras, unsmiling, daring. The colour grey becomes the It colour of the fall season – fashion weeks all over the Western world look like communism.

Then there's the first controversy – a big interview and a photo spread with baby-faced $isi, the tumour girl herself. The photo spread is in *LOVE* magazine – with photographs of various Baldwins and other kids of celebrities – where $isi poses with her chin defiant, her head bald. In one photo she lights up a cigarette – this photo is accompanied by a pull quote in which she announces that her tumour is dead and she no longer fears death. The interview makes the news. There are essays written about $isi being controversial or $isi being brave or $isi exploiting her disease or $isi being irresponsible and a bad example to stupid girls everywhere.

$isi does another interview where she denounces smoking.

It's an old publicity trick: sin, repent. Gloria's PR team is trying to prove they're better at spinning than Piglet was; $isi is their first major celebrity client.

I'm pleased.

* * *

$isi becomes a proper celebrity. She starts getting spotted with various famous dipshits with greasy hair and surfer bods. She is photographed leaving Chateau Marmont early in the morning; five minutes later, James Franco skulks out in a wife-beater, hiding under a toque.

We start to receive movie scripts and hundreds of pitches for products. Products get released. The products are, in order: a fashion line of hats, a M.A.C. grey-ribbon makeup line, sneakers, grey push-up bras, lululemon *Walking Cure* pants and, eventually, the top achievement for anyone in the music business – a fragrance launch. The perfume is called *Grey*, naturally, and according to the press release, it incorporates "Mutsu apple, nectarine, bergamot, rose, amber, blond wood and hot sand." Gloria doesn't find my *this is what cancer smells like* joke funny, but that's what I think whenever I get a whiff of it on the street.

21

MEANWHILE, AS I BECOME MORE AND MORE ABSORBED WITH the campaign, trying to wrap it all up before my contract with $isi is officially up, Gloria decides to say that she's pregnant. She refuses to take the test to prove it, yet insists on an imaginary bulge in her belly. I try not to show my anxiety. Once, I scream into a pillow like a crazy lady in a movie. I want to remind Gloria that she's past forty, but I know that would be insensitive of me, so I keep quiet and pent up. Then, when Gloria gets her period, I try not to show my relief. To celebrate, I go out that evening all by myself and pay a stripper to *not* rub against my new Paul Smith suit while I stare at her tits for the duration of two songs.

The stripper reminds me of Dolores – she is small and much prettier, but she is a mouth-breather and has the same round eyes.

"Can I call you Dolores?" I ask.

"Whatever you'd like, honey," she coos. Her breath smells faintly of alcohol. I don't call her anything. I do nothing when song number three starts.

* * *

After the fake pregnancy, Gloria subscribes to inspirational podcasts telling her to *live in the now*. She dyes her hair even lighter to further resemble her favourite celebrity, Gwyneth Paltrow. She cooks food from Gwyneth Paltrow books; every morning, she swirls coconut oil in her mouth. She becomes allergic to gluten.

She starts doing yoga more diligently, and I often wake up in the morning to the bed empty and sounds of whispery plinking coming from the living room, where she twists her body, her ass in the air, her legs spread, her red face hanging between her legs.

I let her hang a framed quote in the kitchen: *Life is the dancer and you are the dance*. I pirouette in front of it once and bang my shin against the counter.

"Let me tap your leg," she says when I come into the bedroom limping and explain what happened.

I roll up my pants. She taps my leg. "Everything is made out of energy, out of molecules interacting with each other," she says as she taps, her head bent down, hair brushing against my leg. With the desperate new blond shade, her roots seem to be growing out faster – there are many grey hairs among her natural muddy blond. I'm curious about what she'd look like if she were not to dye her hair. I would probably find her aging look exotic – the oldest woman I've been with is Mildred, but she dyes her hair orange.

Right now, Gloria goes on about "the quantum theory of matter and energy being aspects of the same reality" and "life energies flowing through us via a series of paths, known as the *meridian system*, that are mapped out by four hundred acupressure points located on the body," one of them on my shin. Her soft voice, along with the tapping, lulls me to sleep.

When I wake up, it's dark in the room. Gloria is gone. There's a note on the kitchen table that says to try the chickpea salad in the fridge, and she'll be back after her tea-appreciation class.

* * *

Gloria gets a therapist whose job – I hope – is to dissuade her of the notion that there is ever going to be a baby. As she starts to make peace with the idea, she focuses more on Dog. I have to sign forms that allow him to join such extraordinary activities as Dog & Mommy and Urban Dog School classes, as well as Dog Yoga.

An enormous monogrammed Marc Jacobs dog crate is ordered online. Gloria buys Dog outfits made by Prada.

But Dog isn't enough to keep her occupied, and she insists there is still more of herself to be found. She signs up for various meditation groups. Her favourite is mindful meditation, where people learn how to pay attention to their breathing and focus on chewing a single raisin – everything can be combined with reflection; there is wisdom to be found even in bricks that your fingers brush against. Bricks speak to people as do trees and pigeons, and dreams are a source of wisdom. You can go inside your head and find peace there, a haven from what was outside your head; the inside of your head can be an oasis.

There is also a group that Gloria starts attending where she sits in the circle with other women who talk about not having children but wanting them and about not being able to have children, period. Non-moms.

I don't think the group is a good idea – it seems Gloria only comes back sadder and more distressed from it – but I am never asked for my opinion, so I don't give it.

I watch her get smaller and gloomier, collapsing inside herself like those raisins she chews mindfully. I can't get through; the walls of her are yielding but remain impenetrable. There are many mornings when I say, "Is everything okay?" like I'm reciting lines in a movie, and like in a movie, she sighs and looks away and says, "Everything is fine."

One day, I come across a piece of paper where she has written about me, about how much it hurt her to see me moving on with my life after the pregnancy. She calls me "callous, insensitive"; the non-pregnancy is deemed "a tragedy."

I want to say something to her about it, about how there has to be an actual event – an actual lost pregnancy – for it to be a tragedy, but I'm not cruel, not callous, not insensitive.

* * *

I feel panic, then relief when her Non-moms group and her therapist decide that it is time for Gloria to take a break from me because I'm an awful man; a man who is insensitive. There is a part of me that wants to convince her that it's not true, that she and her group are wrong about everything, but I know that my motivations for trying to convince her are only so I could prove to myself that she loves me – that I'm still the kind of man that women love. After the months I've spent focusing solely on Gloria, the weight of her pronouncements seems more significant, dangerous even, to my identity, and I have to remind myself that she is only one woman. And her feelings toward me don't represent how other women feel toward me.

"You're not even going to defend yourself," she says when I say nothing about her calling me names and talking about taking breaks. I am too exhausted by her, by all of this; I am a shell of my former self, to paraphrase a cliché.

"I don't even know who you are anymore," she says.

"Me neither," I sigh, and she must be mistaking my reply for weakness because she comes up to me and puts her arms around me. The image of Caroline, the girl I lost my virginity to, wrapping herself around me to keep me flashes in my mind and I shudder.

Gloria leads me to bed. I make no effort to try to fuck her and she strokes my head, lying in her lap like a kitten, murmuring over and over, "I don't know what to do, I don't know what to do."

I have no idea what she's talking about. I fall asleep because the stroking is nice.

22

IN THE MIDDLE OF SUMMER, GLORIA TALKS ABOUT TAKING a break again – this time it seems that she has made a decision and wants some kind of a plan in place.

I remain passive, my contribution contained mostly to sympathetic – and hopefully guilty-enough-looking – nods.

Gloria says we should "reflect" in August and "regroup" in September to discuss further. Talk about our goals and hopes then. My hope is for Gloria to feel terribly wounded by my continued lack of fight while she's doing her portion of reflecting. My hope is for her to feel so wounded that she will, for example, go to Poland to spite me and reclaim the count who was once in love with her.

"I need more from you," she says.

"Yes."

"I need you to be more present. If you want this to work out, I need you to make the effort. Do you want this to work out?"

"Of course," I say.

"I don't want things to be the way they are. I want us to evolve," she says.

"Me too."

I wish I could tell her why she is wrong about relationships having to move a certain way. It could free her. I always thought she had the potential to avoid succumbing to convention, the way she lives as if she doesn't care about fitting in too much: jet-setting, dating Polish counts, not breaking into my email account to check if I am being unfaithful – stuff like that.

It would help her to realize that she doesn't have to subscribe to the commonly accepted belief that once a couple, we're supposed to move in stages as if we're working for a corporation: giving each other performance reviews (*really good in bed, always calls when he's running late*), expecting bonuses (surprise birthday parties, surprise blow jobs), climbing steadily up the ladder of coupledom (attending weddings, wedding).

I wish I could share with Gloria why it seems so bleak, advancing in this particular corporation – starting with the first weekend together and ending in a shared cemetery plot. How impossible it is to have to remain excited, or at least grateful, or at least not homicidal about the fact that we have to spend most of our adult lives trying to understand a human being that ultimately is just too different to ever understand, the way all the human beings who are not us are.

Then again, we could tell ourselves it is all worth it – it is romantic and natural and even practical. And if we are indeed so lucky to achieve the pinnacle of any respectable couple-corporation, a child, it is okay to die because our work is done. Although, before we go, it is important to instill similar values in our child, teaching her that the only point of her life is to, essentially, pair up with someone, birth something and then die too.

And is modern marriage about love? The love evolving, maturing like some kind of alcohol as it sits in the barrel of disillusionment and misfortune, disease and ephemeral joy? The love maturing so much that it is prone to forgetting that it originated in desire, demanding the same desire to succumb to exclusivity, monogamy? And desire, this chronic viral condition, torturing monogamy with its lips and hips, its swagger and smell, its eye contact, its hands everywhere?

Then, at home, the desire resting next to the wife's sleeping cheek as the husband masturbates in the darkness, quietly, hideously. He is an evolved man, a man who evolved so much that he married, respected and observed the rules of modern society. And later on, his wife locks herself in the bathroom with her secret stash of *Fifty Shades of Grey* or some other romance fable and fantasizes about being mounted by someone else, the neighbour. Anyone but her husband, whom she finds repulsive now, after years of marriage.

I wish I could talk to Gloria about my own parents, stuck in their monogamy. I would tell her about seeing my mother with our neighbour Karl and how they panted at each other, how my father didn't seem to understand – or if he did, never acknowledged it – that his own wife, his soulmate, the love of his life, was separated from her sexual freedom by a metal fence. Then again, if he were to have let her go, he would never have done it to appease her desire – he would've done it to feel smug about it. If anything, he would've done it so that he'd have his own freedom, the freedom to call her a whore for the rest of his life.

It seems to me that the most loving thing to do is to set someone free. Therefore, breaking up with Gloria is a loving thing to do. I have no intention of this being temporary; this is for good.

I lie to her, tell her I'm looking forward to September, when I'll next see her, and she must know that I'm lying because when she leaves my place with her final suitcase, she holds my head in her hands and presses her forehead against mine and says, "Don't ever let a good thing go."

It sounds familiar and it sounds like a threat.

23

I CAN ALMOST SMELL IT. THE WATER AND SAND, THE COCONUT oil and sweat and beer breath. I see the beach in the distance: the whiteness of the shore, the candy-blue of the ocean, the candy-blue of the sky. The freedom expands inside me, along with the salty air. I cannot wait to meet them, all the girls with their wobbly flesh, the straight waists and straight legs and hair fried from home dye jobs. Despite what happened with Dolores, I haven't given up on my passion. I'm still the universal dream boyfriend, and I'm even stronger and more refined this year. I've prepared. In my non-professional life, besides being Gloria's boyfriend, I've also become a secret, late-night teenage-Internet-forum reader, a Facebook commenter, a Twitter subscriber who's been following every rant a plain girl has to post, everything she has to say to the world that makes her mad and invisible. And so now I know even more about boys not returning affections, and how hard it is to find bleach that will work on a moustache without making it stand out if you get a tan. I know more about how impossible it is when dumb hos and bitches steal boys who have been spoken for, how spiteful skinny girls can be, how diets never actually work unless you turn them into an eating disorder.

I know even more about how it would be nice to have someone to care for you, to cuddle with, someone other than the jerks who fuck you and leave you and you have to pretend that you don't care but really you do.

I pull into the driveway of the beach house and turn off the engine and sit in the car with the windows open. In my head, I hear all those voices from the Internet – the squeaky whispers, the whining, the rants – complaining, explaining, asking.

I watch the house, the lifeguard chair in front of it. I want to go and climb it and take in the beach right away, see if I can spot any of them, the actual girls. But then the front door opens and Jason steps out with his new girlfriend with messy tattoos up and down her arms. The ex he was thinking of bringing with him has disappeared. Number disconnected, no emails back. She's probably busy modelling for *Faces of Meth*, or maybe she's dead.

I am impressed with Jason finding a replacement so quickly. Perhaps those PUA meetings have helped him after all, but it was me, more likely, who provided the right inspiration.

Jason found the new girl while giving a workshop to a short-film class at a community college. Candace – Candi – waited for him after the workshop in order to show him a video she filmed in high school. It was about her aunt dying of cancer.

"It was extremely profound," Jason said on the phone. There were long takes of the aunt napping. It was uncomfortable to watch her for that long. "Her face twisted, you could tell she was in pain." He said he almost cried at the end of the film. He couldn't wait to talk to Candi, tell her that she was a genius. He felt an incredible pull toward her, like she was his – like she *belonged* to him, he said. And it was strange, he said, because he hadn't even touched her at that point. He was in love with her brain before he was in love with her body. Once, he ran into Candi shopping with her mother at the market. And even seeing the mother didn't stop him, he said.

"What was wrong with her mother?"

"Everything. She was huge. But that's the least of it."

"Genetics. Well, you're going fully into it then."

"One of those haircuts, short on top. And she was rude. That was the worst. She acted like I was some asshole bothering her daughter. They both smoke. Candi and her."

He only mentioned the mother so that I would remind him of genes. He was hoping that hearing it from me would make him reconsider what he already knew: he was about to embark on a miserable journey to a white-trash nirvana.

At the time of the film workshop, Candi had a boyfriend who was a filmmaker himself. It turned out later that both the aunt and the film were his. But at that point it didn't matter. Jason loved Candi. Candi left her boyfriend. And now she is here, looking at me, eyes narrowing as if we had history – a complicated kind of history.

"So good to see you, buddy." Jason trots over. "Meet Candace."

"Hi, Candace. I've heard so much about you."

"Candi. It's Candi. What did he say?"

"Only good things."

"Really," she says. "I haven't heard anything about you."

She reminds me of someone. She starts chewing on her finger. There was a pretty girl in my high school, Melissa or Missy. She slept with everyone. I didn't sleep with her.

"Yes, you have, baby," Jason says. He's speaking loudly, his enthusiasm put on. There must've been a fight before I showed up. "Candi, this is the guy I told you about. God's gift to women, ha ha."

Candi doesn't smile. She propels herself off the door frame and slinks toward us. I stare back at her. I can't figure out her stare, if it's flirtatious, murderous, indifferent.

Jason meets her halfway and brushes something off her shirt. It's a strangely pathetic gesture. I have an urge to pull him off of her and slap him once, hard, to snap him out of this shameful behaviour, but I know he'd never understand that it's for his own good.

"God's gift to women, eh?" Candi says, extending her tattooed hand: T-R-U-T-H on her knuckles. She winks at me. Jason laughs nervously again.

"Jason is a joker," I say.

"He is?"

Jason fusses beside me, picking up and dropping my bags. He finally settles on a small suitcase, which he carries fussily into the house. I follow him. "Come, Candace," I say.

"Candi," she says.

I don't look to see if she's following me; she is.

Inside, the house is spotless, quiet – perfect, save for the ashtray filled with cigarette butts. The house doesn't smell of cigarettes, so I don't say anything, but I will never invite Jason to stay here ever again.

I don't have a lot of energy left after my long drive. I'm hoping that the lovebirds will leave soon, but I politely sit through Jason's detailed listing of everything that is or isn't working in the house. "We had a lovely time. Got bitten by a wasp when we first got here, but she's tough. She's not allergic – right, Candi?"

"Glad you're not allergic, Candace," I say and she says nothing.

I try to imagine what it would be like to spend three weeks with her, with her overt scorn, those bloodshot eyes. I really don't understand Jason at all. Perhaps he's one of those people who like to be in pain so they know they're alive. A masochist.

Jason prattles on. Candace stretches, her top rising to show another tattoo sneaking out of her cut-off shorts. Flowers or birds, hard to tell.

As they leave, I consider saying something to Jason about getting away from her. But I refuse to act extreme, especially when it comes to sentiments instead of facts. And he would never, anyway. He's smitten.

* * *

My phone rings late in the evening.

"Hi," Candi says on the other end.

"Hi."

"He told me all kinds of stories about you," she says.

"I can imagine." There's nothing more intriguing to a woman than finding out a guy is popular with other women. It's a challenge. An opportunity for a woman to teach me a lesson because, of course, she is different than all of them. She is the one who will destroy me, who will make me fall.

"What can I help you with, Candi?"

"I don't know."

"Maybe there's something?"

"You wouldn't do that to a friend," she says in a voice stretching like honey. Teasing.

"No, you're right. I wouldn't," I say. I try to stifle a yawn, but it comes out anyway and when it does, I think how it's a good thing. It will help things along.

"Do you want to meet at Neon?" she asks. "Jason has a headache. He doesn't want to take me dancing. I feel like dancing."

I picture myself going with her to Neon, a new beach bar that's opened this year. Walking there, she is stumbling because she's already had a lot to drink, and she smells of cigarettes.

We dance, or she dances – she's grinding her skinny ass into me, aggressively; she's laughing with her mouth opened monstrously wide. Soon, she attacks: a combination of aggressive flirting and mocking me for stealing her, my friend's girlfriend. She'd say something crude: *You'd do anything for a pretty pussy, wouldn't you? Betray your best friend, would you?*

And so on. I've never fallen for this kind of thing before. Why would I even bother? Why would I risk my friendship?

I think of Jason sitting in those PUA basements all those years, trying to learn to be an asshole and failing at it. Before Candi, the best part of his day was the part when he'd unwittingly touch himself in his sleep. Once, I saw him approach a *set* of two women, trying to manoeuvre his body so he'd block one of the girls, focus on the other, the less fat one.

I couldn't hear his lines, but I watched the blocked girl – a hipster in big glasses with a curtain of dark hair desperately trying to cover her massive jaw – grow more and more indignant, her body shifting as if to tackle him. Her friend, a forty-year-old-looking blond-brunette in her twenties, folded her arms, one eyebrow pointed at Jason. He was oblivious. He reached out to touch her and she backed away with such disgust and force that he almost fell forward. He turned, looked at me, eyes big and hurt like a child's.

I loved him in that moment, fiercely, like he was my brother. I walked up to the group, eyes on the blond-brunette. The eyebrow pointed at me now. Then it softened. "Give me your number," I said to the blond-brunette.

There was the typical pretend indignation: Why should I? Why would I? etcetera.

"Because you want to," I said. I didn't try hard. She wanted to, of course.

Her friend stared, lips twisted in a ridiculously bright knot. "I like your lipstick," I said on walking away with the blond-brunette's number written on a piece of paper.

I walked up to Jason, standing in the parking lot, watching all of this the way I was watching him before. I threw the piece of paper on the ground. I didn't look back. Jason laughed, and it almost sounded like he wasn't faking it.

"Candace, go to bed," I say into the phone. "I won't tell Jason about this. And if you're smart, you'll make sure he doesn't figure out that he can do better than you." I hang up.

The phone rings a few times, then stops.

The next day, I do my workouts according to my routine of squat variations. I eat a healthy breakfast of porridge with berries, a perfect square of old cheddar on whole-grain toast. I erase Candi's shouty message without listening to the words.

Outside, Dog slaps his tail against the walkway in front of the house. His face is stretched out in an imitation of a smile. I call for him, and we leave for our morning walk.

I don't believe in animals having much personality or character, but I'm sure there is something in Dog that, if he were capable of judgment, would be able to favourably compare being here to being at home with Gloria wearing a pair of Prada booties.

* * *

The beach is just starting to fill up with bodies, and it's nice to be here before it gets too crowded. I take in the surroundings, the endless blue ocean and the horizon of palm trees at the far end of the shore.

I think about Dolores. I think about what it was like walking here with her, how I had missed all the signs of her instability. I think about her body, the way she shuffled even when she tried to run. How excited she was to see the waterfall beside the beach house, how she took her shirt off and freed her pretty breasts triumphantly, on the balcony overlooking the waterfall, for all the world to see. She was so submissive and open, so ready to be liberated from her obscurity, so ready to have the most wonderful adventure of her life and then live her life a little better, in a more enlightened way, having been touched by beauty and luck. Instead, she succumbed to a delusion.

A shiver runs through my body, a vein flash-freezing all the way from my neck down to my groin. Yet this is a perfectly warm, pleasant morning.

I promise myself to be more careful when picking out a girl this time. I don't know how I will guard against failure, but I'll have to keep all of my senses sharp – any indication of insanity and I'm out, no matter how great the challenge, no matter how promising the result.

As I walk, the beach fills with people, and I try to figure out what the summer trends are this year, if there's any-thing that I could get fixated on, anything specific like the colourful string bracelets of last season or the cut-off jean shorts before that. So far, nothing pleasant like that. But like everywhere else, there's one prominent girl trend: shaved heads. *Ribbonheads*. Named after the two heroines of the tumour campaign vlogs, they are girls whose look announces their solidarity with their idol, $isi, and her triumph as a cancer survivor.

Yes, even here, in this world of overfed girl stock who can't afford to go to a more attractive beach, where the fit, intellectual bald girls tend to go. I'd expect a shaved head from a girl who goes to college, who goes to all those other, better beaches – good breeding implies a necessary type of sensitivity – but there you have it; it's here too. I suppose I have myself to thank for the Ribbonheads trend. I'm unsure yet if this is going to be an asset or a liability on a girl. I am fascinated by hair, particularly so-called bad hair – dyed, fried, thin, limp – and lack of hair altogether may be too much, too extreme. I look at all the bald heads around me, but nothing in me responds – my dick remains unimpressed.

24

AS A YOUNG ADULT I HAD AN ACCIDENT. IT WAS A WARM
summer morning and I was rushing to help Jason move his
art from his old apartment to a new one.

I didn't want to help Jason. I wanted to have a leisurely
Saturday, with a beautiful girl I was seeing – this was when
I was dating beautiful girls – someone whom I only recall
as brunette. That's what I wanted to do instead of helping
Jason with his move. But occasionally, I would force myself
to do unpleasant selfless things in order to maintain the
long-term connections that I felt demanded such things;
this is what friendships are like.

I rode my bicycle through the sticky streets of Chinatown,
through a market with its fish smells and bakery smells, all
of it mixed in with garbage and decades of immigrant effort
evaporating from the sidewalks. At one point, I got off the
bike to cross the street. I walked onto the street and felt a
strange tug on my shin.

I looked down. I could see a small, light blue surface poking out of a red gash on my leg. I had walked my front wheel into my own leg. I sliced it open as the wheel turned, cut down to the muscle.

I bent down to hold the wound with my hand, make it close and stop the blood from flowing out of it. As I tried to pull the flaps of skin together over the blue-white fat tissue, something damp and thick fell out of the gash, a piece of meat. It landed wetly on the ground. And it was that quiet-yet-solid wet sound that did it: The world started turning fuzzy, then black, and then it disappeared. The last thing I heard was metal crashing beside me.

When I came to, there were people all around me. I was lying on the ground with a cold compress on my forehead. A voice said an ambulance was on its way.

This is what I dream about my second night at the beach house, about the accident. I wake up exhausted with my jaw clenched, my body clammy from sweat. Even though I don't believe in omens, the sinister way the event has repeated itself in my head, in the guise of a dream, seems like a warning.

* * *

It is in this melancholic mood that I leave the beach house with Dog to go for our walk. We get out later than usual, as it took me forever to get ready: my exercises were laborious, my shower not very refreshing – sand under my eyes.

I couldn't eat much, but I screwed around the kitchen nibbling on things before I gave up.

In addition to my troubling mood, the weather is humid, the sun hazy behind a veil of moisture. The day is an out-of-focus photograph.

I want to check out the smoothie shack, to see if I can find any inspiration there, pull myself out of this funk.

It's not as packed as I expected. Only two Internet stations are occupied and there's no lineup. I order my usual acai smoothie and a bottle of water for the walk back. The bald girl behind the counter seems stoned, eyelids barely lifting as she confirms the order. A zombie. She doesn't smile. But then she does a double take, eyes narrowing as if she recognizes me. I'm used to double takes, but this one is off; it's not curious or friendly.

"What?" I say.

"Oh, sorry. Nothing," she says and turns around. I watch her skinny ass as she fumbles with the smoothie machine. She hums quietly to herself as she passes me the smoothie and water. She hums completely off-key. I want to tell her to shut up, but I'm a gentleman so I say nothing.

I check out the two Internet stations. The first one is occupied by a couple, probably in their early thirties, both dressed in khaki, both with the same dirty-blond hair. They are wearing rubber shoes. One day they will produce a plain child, maybe a girl. Maybe I will still be alive by the time she turns eighteen.

At the other station, there are two girls – one looks a bit like Dolores. As soon as I see her, I feel the anxiety clawing up from the bottom of my gut: What if the actual Dolores is here? But no, she wouldn't be here, I remind myself: that bungalow got sold last year.

I count backwards from twenty. Neutral subjects. Nature, fashion. What to get for dinner tonight. I take a few deep breaths.

The second girl is one of those flawless beauties, with a cute nose and straight black hair that even in this humidity stays silky and flat. Her top is something that looks like a see-through skirt that she pulled up over her breasts to wear as a dress. Her thighs are long, smooth bars of chocolate. An Eight.

She catches me staring. Smile full of bright white teeth; it's the well-oiled smile of someone who gets stared at often. With that, my desire falters and, despite my anxiety, I check out the Dolores look-alike again (noticing, too, the flicker of outrage in the pretty girl's expression as I do).

I take in the clothes that don't really fit Dolores-girl, the chinless, round face. She turns to me and blushes. Too close, too much alike. I look away.

I go outside to untie Dog. Maybe I should just stay in today with *The Sopranos*, which I am finally watching to see what all the fuss was about. Or I could try to tackle the new, complicated contracts Patrick drew up for the Ribbonheads. They are becoming more and more demanding and are threatening to leave. This is actually fine with me, as their job is done – the campaign was successful, and I'm not in the business of representing aspiring actresses.

"Hey," someone shouts.

I turn around. It's the bald girl who served me my smoothie, the zombie stoner. She's walking toward me, quite gracefully for the undead. Her jaw is no longer falling off its hinges.

"Are you that actor?"

This happens from time to time. It hasn't happened in a while, so it takes me a moment to remember that I'm used to it. I get used to it again by the time she catches up with me. "No, I'm definitely not him."

"Are you sure? Aren't you supposed to say no even if you are?"

"Good point. But yes, I'm sure."

"Okay."

"Sorry to disappoint you."

"No, that's okay. Are you sure?"

"Yes. Very sure."

"Alright. I believe you. What's your name? I'm Bride," is what I think she says – *bride* – as she thrusts her small hand forward, and I say, "Sorry?"

"My name is Bride. As in *getting married*. Bride. I know. My parents had a peculiar sense of humour. My childhood was quite traumatizing."

"That's funny," I say and take a closer look at Bride.

She avoids my eyes, which is confusing: this aggressive introduction and then the coyness that follows it. She's almost my height – very tall for a girl – with a thin, muscular body. She's standing ridiculously straight, as if she wanted to further accentuate her almost complete lack of chest.

Her face is all nose, which is not what makes her so strange looking; it is the wide slash of lips that seems to throw her face off balance. She reminds me of someone, perhaps $isi before cancer and before she became $isi and had plastic surgery to make herself more acceptable-looking, cute enough for a magazine cover.

"Had enough?" she says. I can't tell what number she is. Anything between Two and Seven.

"Of what?"

"Checking me out," she says.

I laugh. "Sure. I wasn't. You remind me of my friend's daughter."

"Ooh, pervy."

"What?" *What's wrong with you*, I want to add but don't. This is probably just her clumsy way of flirting, saying offensive things to see if I'll lose my cool. I smile and shake my head as if she were a silly child. She *is* a silly child.

"I'm just joking. Jokes! Sorry," she says.

"No worries. I got it."

"So. You never told me your name," she says.

"Guy. As in *that guy*. My parents had a peculiar sense of humour too."

"Wild."

"You have beautiful eyes," I say.

"Thanks," she says, not at all surprised by this sudden change of gears, the compliment. I wonder if her confidence is actually just a cover-up for shyness and insecurity.

"Is this your dog?" she says.

I nod.

"Beautiful dog."

She doesn't bend down to pet him. Maybe she's afraid of dogs. Maybe she got bitten by one as a child. An image of a grotesque scar, a swirl of valleys of flesh, pops into my head. I try to place it somewhere on her body, somewhere exciting – under her small breast, or the inside of her thigh.

"You can pet him," I say. "Don't be scared."

"I'm not. I'm just not that crazy about pets. I like looking at them, but that's about it."

I wonder if being a dog owner makes me look sentimental to her, or worse, if it says something about me I'm not aware of – like that I wouldn't say no to a placenta milkshake or a yoga retreat.

"No offence," she says, possibly mistaking my silence for hurt.

"Don't you have to go back?" I nod in the direction of the smoothie shack.

She blinks and gives a big toothy smile. "Yeah, I do. I just wanted to say hi, see if you were that actor. Sorry. Didn't mean to bother you."

"No bother at all," I say and make my decision. "Listen," I say.

"Yeah?" She doesn't look away this time. She is nothing like Dolores. But she has that clarity, that sugar in those lovely mahogany eyes that make her look innocent, corruptible. And even though part of me thinks that I might not be the first to have noticed these eyes – that there might've been a boy before me, or even a man who had to perhaps lower his standards just to be able to look into them – I'm willing to take this risk because if that's not the case (another man), then I would like to be the first.

"Would you like to hang out later on?"

She tilts her head and puffs out her cheeks. She says nothing. It's obvious she's trying to play some abridged version of hard-to-get so I help her out, pretend to plead with her. "I'm harmless, I promise."

"Yeah? Too bad."

"Too bad?"

"What's the point of you then?" she says.

"I'll make you laugh," I reply.

"Yeah, don't," she says, and *I* laugh. I laugh because I'm suddenly nervous. She laughs too, then, but it seems out of politeness; it's cut short.

I say, "See? It's working."

She rolls her eyes at me. She rubs herself on her shaved head once in that now-familiar gesture of girls enjoying the strangeness of their baldness, their hands surprised at not getting caught in hair.

"Maybe another time then. It was nice to meet you," I say and start to turn around.

"Don't be such a girl. Be here at seven, okay? Leave the dog at home," she says, and I flinch at the insult, at the rudeness, at being given a command.

I let it go and say, "Great. Seven. See you then," and I snap the leash. Dog jumps on me, places his paws around my waist. We wrestle for a moment, me trying to make him sit back down, him too excited to submit, both of us engaged in a brief, aggressive dance.

"Actually, eight is better," Bride says.

"Sure. Eight," I repeat, sounding a bit too hysterical.

"Okay. See ya then." She walks away.

"Sit," I hiss. "Sit the fuck down." But Dog tenses his back, not wanting or unable to obey. I am not violent, but in this moment I have a hard time not swatting him across his nose.

25

SHE TAKES HER TANK TOP OFF WITHOUT LOOKING AT ME, unceremoniously, as if this were her bedroom, as if I wasn't here. She sits on the bed, scratches her ribbed torso, looks down to figure out what's itchy. I still don't seem to be here. I try to pinpoint exactly when I lost control this evening. Before this evening. Earlier. Probably when I met her, when she asked to meet at eight instead of seven, and like a dumb motherfucker I just said *sure* like I had nothing else to do.

She gets up and jump-dances on the bed to Charlie's newest song. The band has gone almost entirely electronic since the flick they did a song for. It was a smart move for them to abandon their pop rock ambitions and focus on tracks you can really dance to. Just last month, one of their songs got sampled by a popular German tech-house DJ, which gives them cred beyond anything we could've created artificially. A nice ambitious track that borrows from dubstep but without the nasty bass wobble. Overall, Charlie's popularity has risen; there's a line of sneakers in the making already, and one of the Charlie members was photographed having coffee with James Franco.

The robot voice in the song talks about wanting to do things to a boy.

As she dances and jumps, Bride's tiny nipples bounce up and down. I want her to stop jumping, her nipples to stop bouncing even though it's cute.

It's not cute. It's annoying. If anybody saw this, they'd wonder if she was drunk, but no. In fact, she's the opposite of drunk. She is someone who refuses to drink. Earlier tonight, I offered her a drink when we came in after going to the beach, but she turned it down.

"Are you an alcoholic?"

"Ha ha ha. No. I don't drink, that's all."

"Not even a beer?"

"Is this making you uncomfortable that I don't drink?"

"No. Just curious as to why. Most people in their twenties drink."

"I'm barely twenty, dude. Anyway, I don't. I don't like to lose control."

Which is why I don't drink. But I can't worry about that, about her not wanting to lose control. I can probably get her to lose control in some other way. Her jumping on my bed is not her losing control. In fact, it's the opposite – it's her controlling this situation, like a nasty toddler, which I'm tolerating for now because I am a gentleman.

I leave the bedroom to go and make myself a drink. I'm not planning to lose control, but this is one of those rare moments where I think I'd like a drink. When I come back with my vodka and soda, she's lying on the bed, looking up at me, smiling. She's now fully naked. She took her clothes off herself; she wouldn't even relinquish that task to me.

We haven't done much besides some necking when we tumbled into my bedroom – she pulled me toward it, the bedroom, as if she lived here instead of me; she seemed to know exactly where to go, so I let her pull me and we fell through the door – no leading her to my bed to take her apart.

"Like what you see?" she says.

"Very much so," I say.

"Are you thinking about what to do to me?"

I'm thinking about plunging into her, flipping her onto her stomach, biting her neck. I'd pull her hair if she had any.

"Like what? What are you thinking?"

"Let me see you," I say and stand above her, looking down at her little body. She nods. She opens her legs wide and spreads her little pussy with her little fingers, presenting herself to me.

"You're lovely."

"Wanna lick it?" she asks in a small voice, a new voice. A porno voice. Daddy's-little-girl voice.

I set the vodka and soda down on a dresser. She doesn't let go of my eyes as I kneel in front of her. I pull her toward me until her knees are hanging over the edge of the bed. She's got big, bony knees – boy knees. Her ankles are thin enough for me to wrap a hand around each. She smells delicious: sour, hot. I start licking her, parting with my tongue, seeking out the little nub.

She makes a noise, a sigh. I finger her tight little vagina with one and then two fingers, and on it goes, the licking and the finger-fucking, until she starts bucking her hips and pushing my head down. She's breathing fast, "Don't stop, don't stop–" Finally, she tenses as her cunt explodes. She moans. The soft wetness opens and closes around my finger. I keep my finger there until it subsides. My dick is rock hard.

"Give me a second," she says, but I'm not really interested in obeying her anymore tonight. I grab her by the hips and flip her over, gauging the movements of her body, looking for any signs of struggle, but there are no objections; she's happy to be flipped over, and she makes a loud grunting noise when I enter her slick, tight hotness.

She moans and buries her face in the pillow, the back of her bald alien head vulnerable, the sight of it only making me harder and more determined to fuck – right through her if I could. I turn her onto her back and spread her legs as wide as they'll go. "Be a good girl. Open your eyes." I push hard. But she won't obey; her eyes remain closed. A thought flashes through my head: *just slap her.* As soon as I think it, her eyes pop open, and then I feel a sharp sting on my cheek, a quick, efficient slap, her little hand like a blur in front of my face.

I don't know if it's the combination of me thinking it and her doing it as soon as I thought it, or if it's the way her face looks as she does it – unsure yet perversely pleased with herself – but I come hard, the most powerful orgasm I've had maybe ever. I am blown to pieces inside, my body vibrating in wave after wave of pleasure. I collapse on her hot, crazy body. She wraps her legs around me, enveloping me for a moment, her limbs skinny but strong. Like a spider.

* * *

The phone rings so loudly it's as if something detonated in my head. I sit up in bed, disoriented. I try to remember where I am, who I am and what this is. This is Bride in my bed. She is sleeping. Sleeping, she looks like a child. She is a child, actually – well, not exactly, but she's close enough to a child to be called one. I touch my cheek, as if I could feel the imprint of the girl-hand that unleashed such violence on it last night.

The phone rings and rings. I'd prefer to go back to sleep, or better yet, wake up this animal beside me and stuff my dick right in its face, but the phone. *Rrring, rrring.*

I go downstairs. I have to get a new phone. Something quieter. Electronic. Perhaps I could program one of the slower Charlie songs into it, instead of this hysterical ringing. It's one of those ancient things, a rotary with an old-school cradle, a present from Gloria. Not something I'd buy, as I generally dislike old things, so-called antiques, which is just another word for hyped-up trash. This piece of shit has to go.

On the phone, Gloria says, "I know, I know. We were supposed to take a break. I respect that. I'm not calling about that, or I mean, not about us, that's not why I'm calling. How are you?"

"I'm great."

"That's great," she breathes.

"What's up?"

"Believe it or not, business. It's something important."

I know this little trick. It's a girl trick. She's got business to discuss, something *important*, something absolutely needing my attention right away, something that has nothing to do with us but that is something that is extremely urgent, perhaps something like a bomb strapped to her throat and me being the only person in the world familiar with the code on its lock. That must be it.

"You alone?"

"Why wouldn't I be?"

"Okay," she sighs.

I want to go back to bed.

"The campaign. I'm getting even more requests."

"I–"

"And $isi talked to some people and told them about how it was your initiative and now there are some people, some media outlets, interested in doing a bigger story. They want to talk to the guy who thought it all up, you know, give it a personality or something; it's an article–"

"I don't want to give it my personality," I say. It's not the greatest idea. I don't want to reveal that I'm the personality behind anything, especially behind *this*, since it's not really anything I have a lot to say about, other than I just wanted to give $isi a nice going-away gift because at one point I felt it was my fault she got a tumour. And I wanted to make some money off her before being officially fired. So that's the *personality*.

"$isi is pretty adamant that you get the recognition. I mean, brain tumour awareness has skyrocketed. The stigma is fading. The positiveness is taking over–"

"The positivity."

"Right, sure. People think it's really neat that someone had the – had the balls to do – bad analogy, I know – but *the balls* to make it seem acceptable. I mean, it's much bigger than Walk for the Cure – it's another level; people are really pretty impressed. They want to meet the man behind this thing, who wanted to fight the stigma, to change that perception–"

Naturally, people are emotional about tumours. There are many good side effects of the campaign: girls shaving their heads for their sick friends or for their idol, $isi, to show their support, to show that they're all the same. I read all the press about it already, the speculations on what it means for young women to show such solidarity and such sensitivity where normally they just focus on frivolous things: boys and clothes and tampons – but that I'm the driving force behind it all? Nonsense.

"There's a journalist who wants to interview you for an article in *Elle*, not for Brain Tumour Awareness Month because that's in May–"

"I don't think that was my motivation. The stigma-changing."

"And so you told me. But maybe you'd like to change your motivation? Maybe you could be okay, for once, with the fact that you had some impact and that people are fucking interested, no?"

"Are you angry?"

"Yes, I'm fucking angry."

"Is this really about the tumour?"

Silence. Of course not. I know that she was probably pretty excited she finally had a legitimate reason to call me, even though it broke our rule of no contact, and I know that she is not a one-agenda-minded person, that there's always some manipulation going on with her. And, right now, our relationship is that manipulation's drive, the real reason behind the phone call.

"I'll think about it. This article."

"Okay. Are you really okay?"

She probably wants me to say no. She wants me to say that I've changed my mind and that I want to see her, that I want her to have my baby, two babies – or seven! – and that we'll try everything: in vitro and renting out wombs, and we'll apply for a little Ukrainian or a little Mexican just in case, and that I will sell my bachelor pad and amend my ways and become the proper full-time boyfriend that she hopes I will become.

"Yeah, I'm really good, Gloria."

I think of Bride upstairs, all naked, her skin collecting all kinds of moisture from the humid air around her.

"Great," she says, her voice small, so small that it's hoping I will notice how small it is and change my okay to not okay.

"I have to go," I say.

"Yes, sorry. I'll get Trish to call you to follow up."

"How is Trish?"

"She's great. She's dating a really nice guy now, a lawyer."

"Good for her. Have a good day, Gloria," I say and hang up before she says *I love you* or *fuck you* or *I hate you*.

I want to run upstairs. But I pace myself.

I feed the dog. I open the fridge to check what's inside to see if I can get inspired about breakfast. I count backwards from twenty. I count backwards from twenty again.

I run upstairs.

Upstairs, Bride is not in bed anymore. She is standing by the window, holding a piece of paper. I walk up to her, noticing how elongated she is, leanness and smoothness; a space between her legs that filters an entire bar of light that falls on the dark wooden floor behind her and doesn't stop until it reaches the bed. Jason told me a space like this is valuable in the PUA community – a girl with space gets a whole extra point: an Eight becomes Nine. Nonsense.

She turns around. Her eyes are red. "What is this?" There's an aura about her, dark clouds that managed to pass the sun between her legs and envelop her in heaviness.

I take a closer look at the paper. "It's a letter from a girl."

"Why do you keep this shit?" she almost whispers, and I think this is the first time I've seen her vulnerable. I feel relief, even happiness.

"Because I'm a sentimental fuck, that's why. Why do you have it in your hand?"

"Because it was right there." She nods in the direction of my desk. Quite possibly, it was there. But also quite possibly, she had to open the desk to find it, which also makes me happy. But I need to appease. I want to fuck her one more time before she goes.

"I'm sorry, Bride. It was very insensitive of me to leave it lying around. It's just a letter from a crazy girl who liked me too much and who is no longer in my life."

"Dolores."

"Yes, some girl named Dolores."

"What was she like?"

What was she like? "She was just some girl," I say.

"Am I just some girl?"

"No. No, you are special," I say. I realize I mean it. I'm troubled by this.

"Special."

I laugh, I'm not sure why. To pretend that I didn't mean it?

"Oh God. I'm being crazy." She laughs too, and the dark clouds around her part as abruptly as they came on. Her body, stiff and tense a moment ago, goes slack as if someone let a bit of air out of her. "I'm sorry." She walks up to the desk and sets the letter down carefully.

"Don't worry about it," I say, surprised by this change of tactic on her part: first the instant anger, but now this sudden apology.

She says, "I was so excited about meeting you and then we had the most amazing sex ever. I get confused by sex sometimes, by the intimacy. It felt as if we were in a relationship. As if I owned you."

My anxiety is a little bird stuck in my throat, fluttering, fluttering. I swallow, swallow, hoping to drown the fluttering fucker, push it down, make it disappear.

"Wanna come back to bed?" I say, and she nods and walks up to me, naked and sweaty and smelling of sex with a hint of mental illness.

I try not to think how I wanted her to say she does own me. I, too, am possibly smelling of mental illness. I just can't smell it on myself.

I lift her chin and kiss her, still not entirely done with the bird in my throat. Perhaps it's not worth it? My dick has a different idea as it pushes insistently against her thigh, and she presses herself against it and says, "Okay, let's go."

26

WHEN SHE FINALLY GOES HOME, BRIDE DOESN'T LET ME
drive her but instead calls a guy who she says owns a tattoo
shop on the boardwalk. He must be a zombie subordin-
ate from Bride's zombie compound judging by the level
of his barely open-eyed indifference to anything around
him, including Bride. I wonder if they're lovers, but Bride
ignores him too.

I nap the entire day away as if sleeping off a hangover.

* * *

Humans are unpredictable. I'm unpredictable – especially
to myself lately. It's not that my personality has changed.
Personality is not supposed to be fluid. It has relatively fixed
enduring features, enduring traits, traits such as neuroticism
or extraversion. What has changed is my preference, which I
thought would stay unchangeable, like my personality. And
with my preference, my mission to be a plain girl's prince
has changed as well. Or I should say, there's no way I'm

going to be able to be a prince with Bride. She doesn't need a prince. She's crept up on me, her dead eyes mocking me, fixing me in place like an animal being hunted.

But I'm supposed to be the hunter. I *am* the hunter. But not with her. Am I already stripped of my control after ten passive months with Gloria? Was it $isi, her illness, or was it Dolores and her roses, the fact that she found me, that it was so easy to find me? Can anyone find me? Can anyone hunt me?

* * *

In order to regain some control, I decide not to contact Bride right away. It's an old trick to make a girl think you don't care about her. I've never had to use it because I've never cared before, but it comes naturally to me, pretending not to care. I simply decide not to think about her. I'm optimistic about this. Girls respond to being ignored and tend to fall even deeper for you. So that's what I do.

I start preparing a salad for later. Spinach leaves, peppers. A boiled egg. Bacon, crumbled into chunks. Blue cheese.

I take my time. I'm methodical, meditative. I think of Gloria's raisin chewing. I allow myself to not worry about time.

Bride told me she was working at the smoothie shack all summer, though she's not a local girl. She said home was close to the Canadian border; there was a Canadian boyfriend that she lived with for a few months.

The tip of my knife breaks. I think of the kid who sold me the set of the knives – a little pimply twat who knocked on the door of my beach house, and who proceeded to lie about the knives' magical powers, their indestructibility, their lifetime guarantee. The kid joked that the knives should last till the end of the world. Upstairs, Gloria waited for me in the bedroom, naked. The kid prattled on and I told him *okay, okay* and took the box of knives from his hands and signed my name on a piece of paper.

Bride said she's twenty.

"Fuck," I say. I look at the knife. The world will end now.

I throw the knife in the trash.

Bride said she loves $isi and has shaved her head to show her devotion. She owns all of Charlie's albums, even the ones before they went electronic. She didn't say anything about how and if she was impressed with my representing pop stars.

I rummage in the cupboard and find an eight-inch Shun knife that I bought in Tokyo. Nothing will break now. Only the Japanese truly know how to live. I chop. Bride said my other protégé, eighteen-year-old Fifi, is boring but her younger sister listens to her, which is exactly as it should be. Fifi's specifically designed to appeal to thirteen-year-olds; it would trouble me if Bride herself was into her. Her mother likes Fifi, too, which is fine. Mothers are often undiscerning when it comes to music. This is because it's been a while since they cared about anything besides lunch boxes.

The bacon is crumbled. I cut up the egg.

Bride loves movies, especially violent movies. She hates sweatpants.

And now I am going to really stop thinking about her.

* * *

Celia Stone of *Elle* magazine calls and says in a breathless voice that she's been researching the Grey Campaign and is surprised we haven't–

"Mmmhmm."

"So, can you tell me a little bit about the campaign?"

I consider hanging up on her, but I'm bored, having spent my whole day working out, napping and watching reruns of *The Sopranos*. I've even slacked off on eating my lovely salad today. Instead of finishing it, eating it, I consumed a tower of guacamole and arugula with egg on crackers, which is not a terrible snack except that I added too much cumin.

"Guy, is this a bad time?"

"Not really. If you're having fun." I picture her: middle-aged, wide-bodied, carefully outlined makeup, too much of it, kooky haircut (diagonal bangs, multicoloured highlights, that sort of thing).

She coos, "What made you so in tune with people, with what they're going through? The stigma of being *the brain tumour victim* or *the cancer survivor* – I mean, we only have these terms with negative connotations, but now there's this new slew of young people who are fighters, who don't pity themselves just because they're sick or their friends are – I mean, you must feel some kind of responsibility for this. I mean, in a sense, this is a great triumph."

"A triumph?"

"Yes."

"Like I won something in a contest? *What's behind door number three? A tumour!*"

"Sorry?"

"Never mind. Look, there were no noble motives behind this. For me. It's just my job. Money."

Her voice goes a little higher. "You did the campaign because it was *your job*? Because you get paid?"

"Of course. What else? It's just something that we had to deal with. And I had an idea."

"It's a *calculated* move, not some calling that you've had?"

"Leading question."

"I'm just making sure I understand correctly. And Gloria said you're very modest. She said you'd dispute that you felt this great social responsibility."

I laugh. It's funny. It's funny she would say that. But it's predictable she would say that, too, try to make me into a fantasy. "Gloria's delusional."

Celia Stone goes on and on and I say, "Okay," and hang up to check the voice mail. There is a message, but it's from Mark. I delete it.

***

The next few days are a mechanical fulfillment of tasks: workouts, meals, naps, walks with Dog, *The Sopranos*, reading business emails but not replying to them, sleeping – or not sleeping but trying to sleep.

I finish watching *The Sopranos*. It's an interesting show. I can't relate to any of the characters but I like their mumbled talk, their flashiness, their foreignness. The themes of the show are mostly loyalty and revenge. A character named Ralph kills the protagonist's horse. The protagonist kills Ralph. The protagonist's nephew helps to dispose of the body. The whole show follows this pattern: something happens, someone dies because of it, someone kills someone who caused the death, someone else kills the someone who killed the someone who killed the first someone.

I like the young female character, Adriana. She's not someone I would date – too pretty, too exotic – but she's fascinating to watch. Bracelets, fried yellow hair with long streaks of black roots, too much makeup. I am slightly shocked when she dies – it's so matter-of-fact, her death, but that's the brilliance of the show. Because that's how it is in real life. Death just happens – it's rarely spectacular; there are often no warnings.

One morning, my father got up and went downstairs to make coffee. My mother joined him minutes later after putting on makeup in the bathroom. My father was dead, slumped in his chair. According to my mother, the newspaper was opened to the Sports section, which my father never read. That detail became an essential part of the story for some reason. Maybe because there was not much else to say about his death.

* * *

I don't know what to watch after *The Sopranos* – I feel empty, lost – so I pick up a book I've been reading, a novel that Jason's girlfriend left behind. The book is about a girl who has leukemia and will die unless her sister, who's the narrator, donates bone marrow, except she doesn't want to donate any more bone marrow – she's been doing it all her life, getting her marrow harvested, and she doesn't feel like anyone in her family loves her for who she is, only for her marrow. So she rebels, comes to her senses after a teacher has a word with her about her dilemma. I skip some pages. She donates the bone marrow and gets hit by a bus.

I throw the novel in the garbage.

In the evening, I watch some porn online. I'm not abnormally interested in pornography; I don't subscribe to any particular site, but there's always a nice array of free clips on video sites if you search for them: a library of vaginas and dicks and asses and everything that can be inserted, expelled, swallowed and spat out.

Today, I spend a few moments watching a man shoving various objects into a very large vagina: dildos, beer bottles, root vegetables. The video is unsexy; it's like a science experiment you should be able to post on educational websites – showcase the miracles and realities of the grown-up world.

I click on a couple of other videos: a woman in a teenager's outfit pretending to lose her virginity in front of an audience of men and women in cocktail attire, a she-male getting gangbanged by two skinheads, a girl covered in a sheet of fishnet-textured rubber getting her vagina inflated with a see-through vagina pump, etcetera. I am aroused, but I'm searching for a specific kind of performer, so I have to control my urge to rub one out.

I find her eventually: a tattooed *bald* porn star named Belladonna, who lets an ugly man come in her mouth. In my mind, I superimpose Bride's face on Belladonna's – Belladonna is too pretty, too symmetrical. Belladonna is non-verbal, mostly gurgling and moaning, but I have a memory of Bride's voice demanding I come on her face, and in my head I hear, "Shoot it on my face, baby, come on, shoot it." I come.

I have a nap. After the nap, I look for more videos. Find more Belladonna. Jerk off. Turn off the computer. Think of Bride, turn on the computer, find more Belladonna.

I keep looking at the phone, both when it's silent and when it rings, but when it rings it's always the wrong number – it's business, Mark, Jason, telemarketers.

Two more days follow. I jerk off until my dick starts to feel raw. I come up with many excuses for her not calling, invent justifications like an insecure girl: *She got really scared of her strong emotions. She has abandonment issues and doesn't want to get hurt.*

My guess is that she's playing a game, a similar game to mine, where she's feigning disinterest to make me curious. And she's better at this game than I am, even though she has no way of knowing that, because in the state I'm in right now, there's no way she could lose.

27

DAY FIVE: I'M GOING TO SEEK HER OUT. SHE HAS WON.

I show up at the smoothie shack right before it closes. The shack is busy: hordes of girls sucking on straws, chattering, slapping their flip-flops against the concrete tiles, $isi's latest hit blasting on the speakers. Some of the girls are bald; my hands tingle at these false sightings.

She is not behind the counter.

I wait in line, consciously tuning out the conversations around me. The line stalls as usual – some temporary catastrophe has befallen the juicer – then there is a miraculous resurrection and the line coughs and moves forward again.

The ginger-haired boy behind the counter has no idea who Bride is. When I say her name, I realize how dumb of me it was to not ask Bride to see her ID or something to confirm that was indeed her name.

"I don't know any Bride," he says. "You sure she works here?"

"Yes."

"And that's the chick's name? Like *bride*, like she's married?"

"Never mind," I tell him and grab my acai smoothie and push through the cloud of coconut, sun and sweat to surface outside.

I untie Dog and start walking.

I've no idea where I'm going, but as soon as I come across a poster of $isi with a guitar, I stop. The poster announces *An impromptu appearance! $isi's Acoustic Beach Tour.*

Now I recall all the unanswered calls and two emails from Mark letting me know about $isi doing a small spontaneous tour. I recall making a note to reply but not replying.

On the poster, $isi is pictured wearing a white blouse, no makeup. I look closely. The blouse seems see-through but you can't make out the nipples. Her head is smooth like an egg. She's holding a guitar, which makes me wonder if Mark has finally invested in some guitar lessons for her as he always promised. Good for her if he did.

Did she pick this particular beach town because she knows this is where my beach house is? Is this a masochistic manifestation of her leftover attraction to me? I wonder if she'll try to contact me, if she will hang up, if I'll be forced to hang up, if we'll end up not hanging up but talking. All three options are bad.

A tiny claw inside my throat squeezes then lets go. I take a few deep breaths and tell myself to calm down. I calm down.

* * *

When I get to the small stage under a huge white tent, there are people already gathering around even though the concert is not supposed to start for a while. There are security guys everywhere, already. I walk around the white tent to see if I can spot her trailer, but I get stopped by a man as big as a gorilla.

Back in the tent, a tall wooden stool and a mike are set up on the stage. I watch as $isi comes out from behind a white parting in the tent, with a guitar. Her sudden appearance is so shocking that my body doesn't even react to it – no anxiety, no time for it. She sits on the stool and starts plinking away, tuning.

The girls erupt in screams but quickly quiet down. Everyone starts taking pictures with their phones. The security guys form a line in front of the stage, but the girls don't even try to force through. I walk toward the stage. I'm shoved and pushed by hordes of girls rushing from all over the beach.

"She's so real. She's like *real*-real," a lispy blond says to a non-Bride Ribbonhead beside me.

"I follow her on Twitter. She posts hilarious photos. Like the dog that's on the cover of *Vogue*," says the non-Bride. "*Dogue*."

"She really connects with the fans," I overhear another girl say.

I think about the $isi I used to know, a girl who despised her fans and had to drink a gallon of vodka to be able to come out on stage. Dogue. A dog on the cover of *Vogue*. I chuckle to myself.

I can hear $isi clearly from where I stand. Her voice does sound much better than the last time I heard her. When singing, $isi can be playful, and even flirty at times, but she can do wronged like no other. Except this time, the wronged is more resigned; she sounds at ease with what she's singing about. Her real-life experience has finally lined up with things she's singing about: real heartbreak and real pain and some melancholic happiness in there too. There's a new trace of hoarseness to her voice that I guess is the result of her smoky, drinky past, maybe even chemo or radiation. All of that – the way she sings, the way her voice is now – hints at maturity, enough of it to make you believe in what she's singing about.

Right now, she's singing about her surprising lover, which must be about Mark. Possibly about some kind of rape-play they've got going on. Maybe he likes to wear a clown suit to bed. Who knows? In any case, if it's about Mark, I've no doubt that she's surprised – anybody would be to find herself having sex with him. I have no evidence that they're sleeping together. I am unsuccessful in making myself chuckle this time.

I'm glad to see $isi looking so healthy and sounding this good. I've no taste for folky music, which is what this whole thing is verging on (minus the shoes – she's still wearing ridiculously high stilettos), but it works. I suppose I'm happy for her.

I wait till the song is over and then walk back on the beach. At night, the beach is even louder, all lit up with phone screens like fireflies in its darker corners, but mostly lit up from all the bars – so light it doesn't matter that the sun is long gone. It's still hot, only a few degrees cooler.

I see Bride. Even though she's too far away and she's as bald as dozens of other young women here, I recognize the walk, the gentle sway of the hips and the graceful half-bounce of her tall, boyish silhouette.

I shout, "Hey," suddenly unsure about calling her by the fake name she's given me. What a ridiculous thing, that name.

She comes closer, squints. "Hey."

"How are you?"

"I'm great. How are you?"

"Great. I was wondering what happened to you."

"What do you mean?" She tilts her head.

"I never heard from you."

"Oh."

"Well, no big deal. I had a crazy week."

"Yeah. Well, it was nice to run into you," she says and turns around and starts walking away.

"Hey," I shout.

She turns around. "Yes?"

"What's this about?"

"What's what about?"

I say as lightheartedly as I can, "Nothing. I'm just glad to have run into you. Have a good night. Take care," and I turn around.

I walk, half expecting to hear footsteps behind me, but when none follow, I decide that I will need to find a new girl tomorrow. This one is a glitch.

There's a roller-coaster drop in my chest.

* * *

When I get to the beach house, I try to watch television. I flip through the channels like it's my job. I can't seem to find anything boring enough to get stuck on. I get up. I turn on my computer and look for clips with Belladonna. I jerk off.

I try to watch television again.

Next, I sit outside with Dog on the front steps, listening to the distant sounds of the beach, partying. The fresh air doesn't help.

I go back to bed. I lie in bed for what seems like hours, trying not to think.

I get up to look in the trash to find the novel about the girl with leukemia. I have no other ways of putting myself to sleep.

* * *

Bride comes by in the middle of the night. I open the door to her quiet knocking and scratches. She slinks into my hallway and waits for me to invite her farther inside. It's dark on the main floor except for the moonlight coming through the skylight.

I gesture for her to come closer and she does. She is silver, reflecting the moonlight coming through the skylight. We move softly, neither of us talking, and as we kiss, we do it quietly, without any sloppiness or panting.

28

THERE'S NO SINGLE DETAIL THAT I'M ABLE TO FOCUS ON. I want it all. The way her upper lip curls up even when she's not smiling – like mine. The way her eyebrows are thick, dark slashes above those eyes. How her irises expand (coming below me, above me, next to me), how her eyes narrow, making me want to know what has upset her, where she has gone in her mind. (I don't ask. Asking means losing control. But I want to ask.) Onward: her large nose, jutting forward; I like it. Her chin. The small dimple in it – why is even this negative space demanding I not look away? I can't look away.

The freckles. Scattered gold that forms into a pattern but not a pattern at all; there's too many of them.

Her belly, elastic and long; the pubic bone; the severely trimmed puff of curls; her pussy a wet, warm spot mapped out in pinkness and a tint of purple. Her pussy's clicking softness.

Her feet with tendons fanning out as she walks, like strings of an instrument.

We stay in bed for a long time. I ask what her real name is. She says it's Bride. She asks what my problem is.

"Bride?"

"Yes, Guy. Bride."

I don't ask again. I've lost enough control already. We talk. She talks. She talks about her love of films, especially the iconic violent blockbusters: *Taxi Driver*, *Pulp Fiction*, *Natural Born Killers*, *Kalifornia*, *A History of Violence*. She talks about the breakthrough scenes, the characters that made her feel invincible when she'd picture herself shooting a gun, destroying her enemies.

She says, "'All the animals come out at night – whores, skunk pussies, buggers, queens, fairies, dopers, junkies, sick, venal. Someday a real rain will come and wash all this scum off the streets. I go all over. I take people to the Bronx, Brooklyn, I take 'em to Harlem. I don't care. Don't make no difference to me. It does to some. Some won't even take spooks. Don't make no difference to me.' *Taxi Driver*. De Niro."

She's good. I don't know too much about acting, but she's scary accurate, the accent perfectly New York, voice low and dry-mouthed, cheeks half-full of bagel. A little bit like the characters in *The Sopranos*.

"You're funny."

She says, "It was even worse when I was little because I would watch old Bruce Lee movies and think I could do karate. I'd go out and try to start fights with kids in the neighbourhood. They thought I was nuts. They would run away when they saw me coming." She stretches, arms reaching for an invisible star above her, her breasts flat, the tiny nipples. "Mmmhmm, what else? Oh, I braided my hair like Princess Leia, even though I thought she was kind of lame except for the blasters, I guess. My dad was a huge *Star Wars* fan."

I picture her, a slight child with big, serious eyes, the hair wrapped around her ears like wheels of silk. And her dad – her young-enough-to-like-*Star Wars* dad. What kind of dad is he? A dude in shorts with a long beard. Maybe he even owns a skateboard.

She tells me more about her past. It's not a particularly fascinating childhood, but it sounds fascinating when she talks about it. She scrunches her forehead and puffs out her cheeks. She talks with her hands, shaping invisible contours of emotions accompanying stories about mundane events: friends' breakups, a class trip where everyone got drunk, writing an essay about books on brainwashing – *1984*, *A Clockwork Orange* – and winning an essay contest with said essay.

I reach for her hand without thinking, just wanting to touch her. She pulls her hand back. I strain to laugh; can't.

She talks about the small town where she grew up. Similar to the place I grew up except hers was poorer, a single-mom kind of place, a beat-up-sled-and-drunk-Santa-in-the-rainy-November-Santa-Claus-parade kind of place. A shut-down mall on the outskirts of town and a meth problem in a trailer park nearby. Four high schools, all four attended by Bride at some point because she had trouble with girls bullying her over her weird name and her childhood antics – the karate moves, the *Star Wars* hair. Her reputation followed her wherever she went – the reputation of having been bullied, of being the crazy kid – and she had to keep on moving.

"Then I just gave in and became crazy," she laughs.

She graduated and moved to a larger city to study, but then a close friend had a serious accident. Bride dropped out of school. She's not sure why – she wanted out and looked for any reason to justify it. So she told herself she quit out of solidarity and to take care of her friend. She won't say if it's a guy friend or a girl friend, but I guess from the tone of her voice that it was a guy. Was it drugs? Was she romantically involved with a junkie?

She rolls her eyes, "Good one."

She looks familiar for a moment, like someone I dreamt of. It's not the first time she looks familiar. Maybe a girl I knew back when I was a kid. Not someone I slept with. Maybe the familiarity is just because we are becoming familiar.

I say, "Are you planning to go back?"

"Just a minor setback. I never planned to drop out for good. Just needed a break, I guess. Now that I've got some things figured out, I'm going back for sure."

"What are you going to be studying?" I ask her breasts, her perfect tiny breasts, a lick of a curve.

She moves my head when I start kissing her belly. "Film," she says and pushes my head farther away from her body. I stop kissing her.

I've been fucking her for what seems like days now. We talk and we fuck. We sleep. Mostly we fuck and we talk. I can't get enough of either, and I'm able to stay interested to the point of not wanting a break from her.

There's no faltering, not even a whiff of that ghastly breath of boredom. This is no guarantee that it won't happen – boredom has sneaky ways of making itself present.

Right now, everything is so intense I feel like some shaman-ist maniac from India or Nigeria, dancing in flames, but I know there will be no warning when I'll suddenly wonder *what is this for? "Is that all there is?"* Yet for now, I do my best to not think about all that. Gloria would be proud of me: It actually feels as if I'm *living in the now*.

So I pay attention to my now, listen to everything Bride says, fulfill every wish (ice cream in bed, pull her hair, two fingers in her pussy instead of three, etcetera). She doesn't ask questions. In her mind, she must imagine herself an alpha girl, and I let her be one. I let her be the girl she imagines she is.

She talks about books she loves – non-fiction books about serial killers – similar to what Dolores was into – and what she plans to do for the rest of the summer.

"It's a secret project," she says.

"You don't want to tell me?" I'm aware of the fact that asking betrays me again, betrays my desperation.

"Not yet."

"Should I be worried?"

"Why?"

"Given your interest in serial killers," I tell her belly button.

She says, "I can't hear you. What about you? What's your thing this summer?"

"You, actually," I answer truthfully.

"What?" She lifts my chin.

"You," I say. "You're my big project."

"How so?"

"I want you to fall in love with me."

"And then what?"

"And then I'll leave you and never speak to you again," I say, truthfully.

"Ha ha ha."

"You like that?"

"It's cute. Good luck with that."

"What? You don't fall in love?"

"I don't know. I think I was born with that part of me missing. It's just never happened for me."

"I'd like to be the first then," I say, and I lick her shoulder. She tastes of sun. I'm giving away my plan but that's part of the plan.

There is no plan, actually.

"You can try. You're welcome to try."

"You're adorable," I tell her and bend down to stick my tongue in her belly button again, decide this was enough of a break.

* * *

"I guess I want to be with someone who's not boring," she says the next time we talk in bed. A whole day and night has passed with breaks for meals and naps and a few short walks with Dog.

"Sure, me too."

"Is that why you see a lot of girls?"

"What makes you think that?"

"The letter. From the girl. Dolores? And you told me about $isi. And the woman who's been calling you all day today. Gloria?"

"I thought you were sleeping."

"I was."

I like that she's jealous, but part of me is alarmed by how happy it makes me that she might be jealous. A point for me but two points for her because there's no ease in this satisfaction; I shouldn't care, shouldn't even notice – or I should notice, but it shouldn't matter.

"You're not jealous, are you?"

"No. Maybe. But that's natural." She yawns. "Just biology. I'm feeling territorial because we're screwing."

"Territorial," I say.

"Yeah. Why are you biting on my neck when we fuck? Territorial. You're marking your territory."

I pull her hand and kiss her on the inside of her wrist, the delicate web of pretty veins. I've abandoned my usual formulas with this girl. I'm going all in. I'm waiting for some kind of opportunity to infiltrate her more. But I'm making mistakes: I'm asking too many questions, and I want to hear her answers, and she knows I want to.

She says, "I like it that you appreciate women. I know you might not believe me because of that letter. But honestly, I rarely get possessive," she says.

I know you should never trust a woman who says she doesn't get possessive, but I'm starting to think not a lot of conventions apply to Bride:

"I like a variety. I'm being healthy about it." I'm not letting go of her wrist. And she doesn't try too hard to pull her hand away. She sighs as I lick her there, gently. Her skin is hot; I can feel the microscopic pulse of the veins against my lips.

"Yeah, me too. I'm healthy about that too. I don't need to prove anything," she says, and I have to wonder: how many lovers, realistically, could she have had? But then again, if she has the same effect on the rest of the male population as she has on me, the count could be quite high. And a girl who knows her value, who understands her power, is a hundred times more powerful than I could ever be.

The sad thing is, many girls pervert this power by becoming demanding, impossible to please – or worse, they let some asshole tell them that they're not all that. Then they spend the rest of their lives looking for validation – in diets, in more inadequate boyfriends, and later, in children, in plastic surgeries, in who-has-more competitions. If it wasn't for men like me, many of those women would never know they're worth more than they think they are.

"What happens when you meet someone?" I say, as light-heartedly as I can.

"Oh, they like me, I like them a little bit. They cry, I don't. You know, same thing you do. I leave. They all turn boring eventually. Well, not even boring, not all of them, but predictable. I mean, sooner or later, something comes out, some kind of bullshit, some hang-up, and I get stuck with having to be the caring, loving girlfriend. Which I'm not. Not at all."

I wonder about the friend she dropped out of school for. I wonder if someone took advantage of her sticking around for too long. If she got trapped with some sad-eyed loser. If she found herself betraying her free spirit. I wonder if this is just bluffing. I wonder too much.

I hope she's not bored with me.

* * *

Eventually, we take a longer break to eat something substantial. I'm happy to be in the kitchen. My body is pleasantly woozy from all the fucking and lying around. I make a Moroccan-style spicy chicken sandwich with tomatoes, olives, almonds and a tomato-currant relish.

Bride eats silently, methodically, as if this were a task. In bed, she's sensual and playful, game for anything I ask her to do. Here, she's just masticating. I've seen her type of eater before, one who eats just because she needs to get it over with, not necessarily unappreciative of the food, but unable to appreciate the pleasure of eating.

"Very good," she says when she's done. She shakes her foot; her flip-flop, hanging off the toes, does not fall off. "Cunt," she says quietly.

I take my time with my own meal. I chew slowly, letting every bite expand into its full flavour. I love the smooth, springy texture of the olives. I suck the juices out of the morsels of meat. The crispiness and smoothness of the almonds, the sweet, sour kick of the currants.

She continues shaking her foot. She sighs.

"You okay?" I say.

"I hate slow eaters," she says.

"I hate children," I say.

* * *

She puts on a little summer dress. We go outside. I feel myself sobering up. In my head, questions demand to be answered.

"What happened with the smoothie shack?"

"It wasn't my thing."

"When did you quit?"

"Maybe the night I met you? But don't worry, it has nothing to do with you. The place sucked, that's all. Why?"

"I asked the kid who worked there about you and he seemed surprised. He laughed when I asked for Bride."

"How many times are we going to go over this? You wanna see my ID?"

"No, of course not. I believe you. Listen, I'm the guy with *Guy* for a name, so I should talk. You okay?"

"Yeah. Okay. Sure."

"I didn't mean to upset you."

"You didn't. But stop bringing it up. It's weird. You're being weird."

"Sorry," I say. I've never been accused of being weird. It feels gross. And the fact that I just said *sorry* feels small and desperate.

We walk in silence. The beach is full of Fours and Fives, but I can barely focus. Bellies and nipples and asses and knees and hair. A parade of body parts. Nothing stands out.

Bride's bright voice snaps me out of it. "We could be like sexual *Natural Born Killers*. I could find girls for you," she says. She grabs my arm. We stop, facing each other. Her face is flushed. "Instead of killing people, we'd fuck them."

"Right."

"I could really help you," she says.

"Help me."

"I'm gonna bring you the girls and you can do the rest."

"Hilarious."

She almost shouts, "I'm serious."

"Okay."

"I'd befriend girls and then bring them over so you could have fun with them, you know, fulfill your endless appetite. For variety. Virgins for the dragon."

"You are crazy," I say and try not to think about Paul Bernardo and Karla Homolka, the serial killers Dolores was fascinated with. Is that how all of that started?

I have to bend over and place my hands on my knees. While doing this, I think up a fantasy: Bride in her girly dresses, talking to other girls, holding elbows, heads touching, bald heads and hairy heads in the sun, laughing, chewing on straws in their drinks, spraying liquid out of their noses, Bride bringing them over to my lair, music pounding, everybody, all the girls, jumping on my bed.

"Guy?"

"I'm good." I straighten up, start walking.

She trots along; tiny feet, tiny steps. "No, but seriously, eh? Don't you think that would be cool?" she says.

"How would you know what I like?"

"Oh, I'd know. I'd figure it out eventually."

I imagine taking Bride for one of my walks, showing her what I'm looking for, teaching her to observe and notice the specific plainness: the girls that look as if someone just slapped their features together, fat asses or asses that are flat like a pancake. She'd be hurt to learn of these girls, I'm sure. She'd wonder if she had the same appeal to me, and I'd have to explain that she hadn't, in fact – well, maybe just barely – and that her appeal is not of the same sort. *It might've started that way*, I'll say. *But that's all.*

"What about her?" She points to a group of girls, her age or maybe younger. "The one in the green bikini."

I isolate the one in the green bikini, and she is curvy, with hair like a sheet of burned gold, mouth full of lips and teeth, but perfectly proportionate.

I shake my head.

"Seriously, Guy. *Look* at her," Bride says. I pay attention to her voice. Nothing in it suggests she's getting upset over this. It doesn't sound as if this was one of those girl tests, checking what or whom I'm attracted to so that she can twist it into a fight.

I say, carefully, "No. Not my type. Perhaps the other one, the one in the stripey one-piece."

"What? *Her?*"

"I don't know, there's something about her," I say.

"She's a fucking fire hydrant. I'm sorry."

"Yes. That's why I like her. Take a closer look."

I wait. I wait for her to observe the girl carefully, and she does. I watch her eyes zero in on the girl. I bend down to stroke Dog's bumpy head.

Bride sighs, "She's just so—"

"Yeah," I say. "Plain. That's it. Let's go," I say, and pull her along.

We walk all the way to the end of the beach in silence. I watch Bride looking at groups of girls and couples and individual girls around us, and I imagine my eyes seeing through hers, seeing through the awakening of her eyes. I imagine my eyes blending with hers, teaching them to see what I see.

* * *

When we get back to my place, we both drink a glass of vanilla-protein smoothie.

"Tell me more." She sets her glass down.

"Okay. It's like a fetish. But not quite. They're not essential to my fulfillment of sexual pleasure. It's more cerebral. It's all about me, but it doesn't work if they're not involved the way I need them to be."

"So you want these girls to worship you?"

"Not exactly. You see, a girl like that, a plain girl, would never have a chance to be with someone like me, right? I mean, I know it's arrogant, but I'm simply stating the facts. Beautiful women often pair up with unattractive, plain men. It's not fair, but it happens. Why does it happen? Because of power, money, control. A beautiful woman wants control and money and power, and he wants her beauty. They work out an arrangement and everyone is happy. But what about a woman who's not attractive? A woman who's not only unattractive, but has no other power? A girl who is not yet formed, but who already knows enough about the world to not let herself have any hope about her ability to attract guys, interesting, smart, attractive guys? You see, if I give her the illusion that it's possible for her to be desired by someone beautiful and successful, I may open her up to so many possibilities, may even give her enough boost to do something interesting and powerful with her life –"

"But what makes you think that she won't anyway? This is bananas." Bride doesn't sound angry.

"Yes. Yes, she might. But sadly, the world values women based on their looks, and sadly, most women base their own value on looks. So I'm just responding to that, nothing else.

I bring joy to girls who would otherwise have to wait for joy for a long time. Maybe forever."

Bride's big brown eyes scan my face cautiously. But I can't stop now. "It gives *me* great joy to awaken this in them. I delight in knowing that I'm their first love – this doesn't happen every time, of course, but still, it happens. It's a lovely thing, Bride. I enjoy knowing that they go out into the world feeling like princesses. Feeling like they could do just about anything."

"You think they feel this because of you? You seriously think this way?" She's not raising her voice or making any ugly faces when she says this. She says this with the same calmness as when she asked me for a vanilla-protein smoothie.

"Why not? Why shouldn't I believe it? Bride, look at me. It's a dick thing to say, but I'm a catch, don't you think?"

She gives a little smirk.

"Why do people always shit on those who admit to being awesome? I'm awesome, and I won't let people shit on me – what's wrong with that? And I believe that I was put on this earth to bring a few girls some great memories, some happiness even – what's wrong with that?"

"Nothing. Nothing's wrong with that," she says.

"I hope you mean that. I really do. It's important to live honestly, don't you think? To live in a way that's closest to our nature."

"Yeah, sure. I guess it's refreshing." Her are eyes down.

I worry that I've said too much.

But how could I have said too much? I just told the truth. Fine, she can hate me for it, for admitting who I am, but that's on her and not on me, and there's nothing I can do about it now.

"I'm going upstairs. I apologize if I've offended you. That was not my intention," I say. I go up to her and give her a quick peck on the cheek. She's stiff, but she tilts her head to receive the kiss.

I go upstairs without looking back. She'll probably leave now. I expect her to leave. I've offended her. I enjoy having her around, but perhaps I've overestimated her level of comfort and understanding. Also, I'm hurt about her rejecting my philosophies. At the same time, this could be a good start to my detachment process.

The door clicks gently downstairs. No big deal.

I go downstairs to see what the house looks like without her in it. I take the empty smoothie glass out of the sink. I throw the empty smoothie glass against the wall. It explodes, shards and milky bits flying everywhere.

Now I finally know what it's like to throw a glass against the wall.

29

I DREAM OF RUNNING THROUGH A DARK, MOSSY FOREST, MY paws and my face covered with grit and stickiness, my fur filled with breeze, my fur like breeze itself, nothing like what I'd expect fur to feel like. My fur filtering the nightly heat, cooling me down as I run and jump over broken branches, step on wet grass, bounce off of rocks sinking in marshes.

The moon is full. I run. I brush against the raw bark of trees. I feel my skin getting torn by something sharp that grazes my side in a narrow passage between trees, but I don't stop.

I see in the dark; my nose can see in the dark. I see everything; I *see* with every sense in me. My teeth are bared and the wind smashes against them; my fangs are like antennae, feeling out the next pulsing artery somewhere in the distance, ahead of me. My mouth is wet, soaked. Blood. Most of it not mine. It mixes with my own blood, pumping into the fibres of my muscles, muscles so purposeful they're shaped like wings, thousands of wings interlocked with one another, making me speed ahead, making me fly, till I crash mid-flight, falling...

Falling...

***

I'm awoken by a creature, a succubus, straddling me with slim, strong thighs. One narrow hand clamped over my eyes, the other hand reaching down to pull my dick from under her ass, and as she does, her hand over my eyes moves slightly and I see her, my bald-headed demon bride, my belladonna.

She inserts me inside herself. She moves steadily up and down, exceedingly fast, thighs tensing and releasing. I reach for her hips to try to slow her down, impale her further onto me, but she pushes my hands away, shakes her head no. Her face is blank, it's a mask, and up and down like a machine she goes. The first waves of pleasure well up deep in my lower abdomen – I struggle to remember something mundane, something to distract me from too-early release. Someone. The journalist who called to get the Grey Campaign story. What was her name? I picture her how I imagined her: a big, wide body. Celia.

My mind does its own thing. Big Celia. She's splayed out on some couch. She's wearing beige stockings and nothing else. Her mascaraed eyes are closed and there's a hand going in and out of her inserting bottles, vegetables – and I have to stop and quickly multiply twelve by fourteen, which is ten by ten, which is one hundred, and then two more tens and four more tens, which is sixty on top of one hundred, is that correct? And two times four, which is eight, so that's one hundred and sixty plus eight, so that's one hundred and sixty-eight –

"Guy, Guy." Bride's voice breaks through, shattering my hundred and sixty-eight into mercury pellets all over my brain.

"Guy, baby," she pants. She has stopped moving and she's just sitting with my dick inside her. She's giving off a scent, hot tartness and salt and something else, something extra that's not entirely human – residue from a muddy run through the forest.

"What you told me. It's a great idea. The girls," she breathes loudly.

"Oh."

"Yeah, yeah. It's fine, so good." She moves up and immediately bears down. Our groins are a swamp of sourness that's pouring out of her. I won't be able to hold for that much longer.

"But I want you to do something for me. I have a strange, ah, *thing* too. I want you to –" she says, and goes up again. Six times thirteen is sixty plus six times three –

"I want you to choke me," she says. "You told me yours, so I'm telling you mine." Now she's not moving at all.

Choke her. I reach with my hands and pull her down, pull her closer to me. "How do you want me to do it?" I feel her pulse around my dick, just a tiny wave of muscle squeezing, like a wink.

"Just put your hand around my neck and squeeze. Keep going until I give you a sign. I'll close my eyes. Stop when I do. I don't actually want to die." She giggles a little. "Don't give me that look. Trust me," she says.

"I need to trust you so you won't let me hurt you?" I say.

"Exactly." She gets off of me and lies on her back. She moves her hand slowly above her beautiful, stretched-out, moonlit body, presenting herself to me.

What if I *won't* know how to stop, *won't* be able to control myself well enough? What if something springs out of me and tries to attack her, tries to kill her once I unleash it?

She moves her hips, pulling me deeper. My mind is filled with images from my dream: running through the forest, face covered in blood, speeding, feeling the wind wrap around me as I gain momentum. There's tingling, electricity gathering deep inside me.

She stares back at me. She nods a small nod and I wrap a hand around her tiny neck. I feel the gentle swell of her throat underneath the pad of my palm.

I tighten my grip.

She gives another nod. Tighter.

I go tighter. I feel her throat contracting, a worming movement underneath my hand as she swallows.

She gives another nod.

My grip is really tight now. This might bruise her, so I loosen my grip a bit, but she shakes her head and mouths *don't, don't.*

This is a satanic challenge. But I know she wants to see if I'm capable of meeting it, if I'm at her level, if I'm not boring. I imagine dozens of little boys before me panicking, stopping, or worse, fuck-this-shit stopping, or worse still, telling her to get the hell out, calling her a freak.

I don't want to be a disappointment. I can't be a disappointment. I want to be her first love. I want to be the one to break the spell, make her fall for me, whatever it takes.

So I tighten my hand around her neck, my fingers digging into her skin, too deeply now.

She grimaces but I keep tightening my grip. I feel my nails breaking her skin and I imagine I feel the wetness, blood, seeping from underneath my nails and I tighten –

She closes her eyes then, slowly, like a doll. A smile spreads on her face.

I loosen my grip, and it's as if I'd been choking myself too – my whole body uncoils as relief comes over me.

Bride gasps and coughs, then just breathes loudly, bringing her hand to her throat. She tenses her lower back and thrashes backwards, her cunt spasming and contracting, squeezing me and drawing everything out of me, milking all the cum right into her – which is when I realize that I'm not wearing a condom this time, which should deter me but just makes me come harder. As I come, I have some kind of a half hallucination of something primitive, primal, an egg exploding into a fetus, birth splitting open our united bodies, shattering my entire being into a powerful orgasm.

I collapse on top of her. In the semi-darkness I see Bride's eyes flicker, something behind them coming apart, loose, some kind of sadness, though maybe I just imagine it. We lie there, next to each other, cooling off, not talking.

I fall asleep with my arm draped over her flat stomach; in my dreams, the furry animal that is and isn't me is digging up a burrow somewhere in the forest with the moon shining on.

30

THE PHONE RINGS AND I REACH FOR IT, CLOUDY WITH SLEEP.
The morning light is sharp, knives in my eyes.

"Hello," Bride says. In the phone, not beside me, which
is strange, but then again, she's a strange girl, so I just
say, "Hello."

"Sleep well?"

"Yes. I had the weirdest dream," I say, looking at where
her body left a whisper of an imprint on the sheet.

"I'm wondering if you could meet me on the beach," she
says in an oddly businesslike tone.

I don't mind that she doesn't want to be flirtatious on
the phone, so I don't push my dream chat – I just ask what
time, and she says as soon as possible.

Then I remember the condom. "Is this about the condom?" I say.

"How about you meet me in an hour?"

There's a pill a young girl can take within the first forty-
eight hours. I have no clue if a pill like that is available over

the counter or if we'll have to find a hospital where they can administer it. I don't know if she's old enough or if she's too old for it. I already dread the wait in the clinic and whatever else, a possible lecture from a gynecologist, some mustachioed local doctor with a degree from a university in Nassau or Zagreb.

I should maybe call Dr. Babe. It would be good to bring an actual woman that I fuck to her; maybe it would finally intrigue her the way my asking for tests never seems to. An actual woman might make things real. I feel like Dr. Babe is the type who likes a challenge – after all, she finished medical school, and that is a very challenging thing for a girl.

Bride says, "By the smoothies. I'm picking up a couple of things from there."

I say yes and hang up. It's going to be a nice day today according to the Internet, twenty-seven degrees and a breeze. A fantastic day to spend on the beach, and even though I find it impossible to sit on the sand for long stretches of time, I imagine going with Bride and lying side by side, discussing the girls that walk nearby, unaware of our predatory eyes.

I don't have time for a long workout so I do a super-thirty, multi-interval: jump rope, diamond push-ups, Hindu squats, leg thrusts, kick lunges. I go fast and hard to quell the anxiety that for some reason has reared its head again.

I take a cold shower, so cold that my head feels numb and there's pain in my ankles as the water cascades down my body. After drying myself off and putting on skin lotion, I put on a clean white linen shirt and linen pants. I skip shaving since it's day three. I've been told a thousand times how great I look with my near-beard. It's my summer look.

I let Dog out in the backyard to do his business. I make a mental note to scoop the business later to keep the raccoons away. You don't want dog shit in your yard ever, or you'll end up with all the shit-eating animals taking over.

I grab a bottle of vanilla-protein smoothie, the last bottle left in the fridge, and I gulp the entire thing. Then I lock the door and walk toward the beach, the liquid sloshing uncomfortably in my belly.

The sun is pale. It's not even eight a.m. In the distance, the closed shack looks haunted, like a place that's been abandoned for decades because of a deadly virus. They should repaint it.

I see Bride sitting on one of the picnic tables out front. She is facing the water. I get hard as soon as I notice a flimsy yellow scarf around her thin neck.

She turns and shades her face with her palm. "Hey you," she says.

"Hey."

"Sorry to get you up so early. I thought of letting you sleep in, but then I thought it would make more sense if we got this out of the way."

"Got what out of the way?" I bend to kiss her, but she moves her face away. She coughs. Then she looks at me and smiles a sad little smile.

Perhaps it's how fond I've grown of her over the past couple of days, perhaps I failed to see this all along, but now I can tell that her charm truly comes out when she smiles. Despite the facial asymmetry, her mismatched nose and lips, she's one of those women who blinds you with beauty as soon as you tell her a joke she likes. She's the kind of woman for whom you will long madly, possessively, as soon as she stops laughing, and then all you'll ever want to do in life is make her laugh again.

I want to tell her this. I also want to tell her to never get a stupid nose job, never let some idiot tell her that she would be more perfect if she inflates her lovely breasts with silicone, but I keep quiet, waiting for her to talk, something uneasy slithering its way down my back as I stand waiting.

"Thanks for coming. Though I guess in a minute you'll wish you'd stayed home," she says.

"What do you mean? I'm glad I came. I'm always happy to see you."

"Okay," she says and shrugs. "Have you ever really punched anybody? Like when you got angry at them?" she says, and I immediately think of our bedroom games. Will I have to punch her next to prove myself to her? The chill on my back doesn't let up.

I count backwards from ten before answering. "The choking was your idea."

She nods, her eyes still, unblinking.

I have a sudden image of crows, a field of crows. Like in that painting by that lunatic.

She says, "Yeah. But would you do it on your own? If I said something that really pissed you off? If I told you something horrible? Or not horrible, just, um, something that could potentially cause a violent response?"

I don't know what she's talking about, but my body seems to. The thing slithering down my back grows colder, expands. I think how the scarf wrapped around her neck is not one solid colour; there are thin red lines popping out of the yellow – it looks like a splash of egg yolk with bloody threads dissecting it. Her hand flies to the scarf as if my eyes made it burn.

"What's going on, Bride?"

"Guy. It's *not* Bride, actually. Why would you even think that's a real name? Seriously. Come on." She bites on a cuticle and spits it out. She kicks a small pile of dirt with the tip of her pointy flat.

"What is your name?" I ask, my back too stiff, hardened with ice.

Her eyes on me. "In a moment. But it's not Bride. First, I need to tell you about why we're here. I'm about to tell you something that will make you want to hit me, which would be okay since it could only help me further, or rather further my cause, but I don't want that. Contrary to your impression of me, I don't like violence. Can you have a look?" she asks, and sticks out her throat so I can open the scarf.

As soon as I graze the flimsy texture with my fingers, she thrashes her head and screams. She screams and then she stops. Then she laughs. The laughter right after the scream. It doesn't fit.

"What the fuck is wrong with you?" I say, but my voice breaks and it comes out in a squeak. I'm shaking. I'm suddenly unable to stop shaking.

"*Bride*. It's the name of a character from Quentin Tarantino's movie *Kill Bill*. Look it up."

I lean against the picnic table. She turns her face toward the water again. We probably look like a nice couple, up so early, so healthily, out for a nice walk, taking a break.

She turns back to me. "Listen, in a minute I'm gonna leave. I'm gonna walk all the way to town and walk right into the police station. It's not a far walk, but it's far enough and it's important that I get there looking a little beat. I'm gonna to go in there and tell them that I've been sexually assaulted and that you did it. I haven't taken a shower yet because I figure we're gonna have to go to the hospital to work up a rape kit and all that. I'm gonna call my daddy and my mommy and tell them what happened, and I'm gonna cry on the phone. They're gonna tell me it was a bad idea to work at the smoothie shack in this shitty little place, but other than that, they won't say anything mean because they'll feel very, very sorry for me. As they should. I may or may not suggest that you were trying to kill me, I haven't decided yet. I'll probably have to–"

"What the fuck is wrong with you?" I squeak again, and I can't come up with anything better than this. My mind is a field of crows pecking and pecking and cawing, cawing, cawing. I feel nauseous.

"I don't know what's wrong with me. I've always been a bit unusual, I guess."

"But why? Is this a game?" I say, and the cawing is so loud now I can't hear my pathetic squeaking. Everything around me becomes strangely large, towering over me. She's a monster, a Godzilla with red eyes, and she's asking me to choke her and my hand is on her throat and her eyes open and then it's not her–

She says, "Dolores."

– and so it's not her, it's Dolores, Dolores underneath me, and I'm choking Dolores, and she thrashes and her face is a grimace, a death face. I can't stop choking her and she dies, and her eyes open wide, round, wide sugar eyes, and it's too much to look at.

Dolores?

"Dolores?" I say.

Bride nods and says, "Yeah, Dolores. My friend Dolores," and her face softens. She transforms from Godzilla back to a girl, a child. Her face – I don't know, whatever *beatific* is, this is it. So young, so sweet, almost glowing from the inside. Holy. Beatific. Not like last year.

Because now I recall her, her *other* face – her scorn and the long, dark hair when I met her for the first time. Her name is Emily. Em. I try to remember if we talked then, but we didn't because I would've remembered it.

I want to say something, but what could I say?

I just watch her. I watch her and say nothing.

She gets up and walks away. Walks all the way to the police station, I guess. Maybe she crawls there for all I know, to appear even more beat up.

Maybe I should run after her to stop her, stop this craziness, but I don't.

I feel like throwing up, but nothing comes.

31

I DON'T REMEMBER STAGGERING HOME, BUT I MUST'VE STAG-
gered home. It's not a far stagger. Once I get there, I fall
through the front door and close it and lean on it as if
that could actually fortify me against whatever is coming.
I should call my lawyer.

I don't call my lawyer.

I think about getting in the car and driving far away. But
I'm no match for the officious, angry cops in every shit town
across this state. I picture myself flooring the gas, sweating
despite the a/c, crying and cursing her name (her real name),
only to get stopped by Officer Fuckstick in Buttfuck, South
Carolina, population 1,000. How appalling.

I picture myself falling out of the car, babbling on, unable
to control myself like a little bitch. What am I supposed to
do when they come? What is the appropriate thing to do if
you're an innocent person accused of a crime? If you're a
person who will never actually get proven innocent because
of the victim's superb acting abilities? And I have to give it

to her, she is a wonderful actress, putting on movie mono-
logues just like that, with the right intonation and look – my
little *Taxi Driver*, calling herself a crazy film-related (too!)
name, convincingly enough that I keep forgetting to ask for
ID, pretending to work in a crap job just to trap me.

I count from a hundred down to one and then from fifty.
The nausea doesn't subside, but at least it feels as if I'm trying
to help myself. I have no clue what else I can possibly do,
so I decide to cook.

I will make a summer vegetable ragout with curry sauce,
which is not a complicated dish, but it requires an array
of ingredients.

As I prepare the ragout, I begin to relax, settling into the
familiar choreography of opening, pouring, stirring, chop-
ping, mixing.

I mix two tablespoons of oil in the saucepan. I pour in
carrot juice and briskly stir the mixture until it achieves
uniform consistency. I don't have some of the vegetables the
recipe calls for. I'm missing fresh corn and summer squash.
I only have enough for one cup of arugula, slightly past its
best-before date.

I could call my delivery guy, but I don't want him inter-
rupting the police.

At this time, my curry sauce is ready to be turned off and
drained. I pour the mixture through a fine strainer over a
bowl, squeezing all the solid matter. I season the curry with
salt and freshly ground pepper and set it aside.

The phone rings.

I put down the eggplant I'm holding. I like the feeling
of its slick, rubbery skin.

I pick up the phone. The police say I should come over. Clever girl.

* * *

The two cops are unfriendly but polite. Just like cops are in the movies. The first cop is short. He has a moustache. (There must be a rule that requires a certain percentage of cops to grow moustaches, one in five or something like that.)

The room I'm sitting in is pale green, almost white. A door with a thick glass window. Like in the movies, there's a camera in the corner of the room. I think, absurdly, about waving at it.

There's a metal table. (Probably issued from a cop movie as well.)

"What's so funny?" asks the younger, taller cop with no moustache.

I shake my head, cough.

He asks me, again, if I know Emily Rose Reese.

"I do," I say, although that's not Emily Rose Reese, the girl they're asking about. Emily Rose Reese is the weird girl I barely remember talking to last year. A blur of annoying quips and thick brown hair, lots and lots of thick brown hair, and glasses. *Em.*

The moustache says again, "So you do know Emily Rose Reese?"

I don't know Emily Rose Reese. Em. I think of the yellow scarf, capillaries of red breaking through egg yolk. The red of her eyes as the sun pierced through the irises.

"How did you meet Ms. Reese?"

"There's a kennel number on the fridge," I say.

"Pardon me?" says the moustache.

"It's not for my lawyer. It's for my dog. Someone should get him," I say, and it occurs to me for the first time that we are not in the movies. This is really happening.

I imagine her crying and shaking, showing off the bruises and scratches on her neck, wincing theatrically when people come closer to have a look. I imagine someone asking if it's okay to take a picture, a no-nonsense but friendly female cop squatting beside her, telling her that she's being very, very brave for doing this. And she's looking up at the female cop as she says in the tiniest voice, *You think so?*

I know so, the female cop says, and her face is complicated; it shows admiration (for Emily Rose Reese) and disgust (for me) – kindness and toughness all at the same time, all needed to express the proper kind of support for the victim.

Later on, Emily Rose Reese will open her legs, allowing people in white coats to insert swabs into her and take samples to keep in red bags with black biohazard signs against red squares. I want them to be gentle with her, those people, to scrape and pinch and whatever else they need to do but *only* as much as necessary. I suppose I should wish her harm, someone ripping open her cervix in some horrible accident (an earthquake could cause a slip of the hand), but I don't.

I realize now that I was Emily's, Em's – Em; she's *my* Em – mysterious summer project. It's comforting to know that I was indeed that important to her if only for a little while. But then not just for a little while, really. This, what's happening right now, *this* is bonding. This is for life, her accusation and my supposed crime. I will always be the perpetrator, from now on, and she will always be the victim. We will be forever linked in the eyes of the law and the rest of the world. Suddenly the name *Bride* doesn't seem so out of place anymore because this union of ours is a marriage; it was for better and now it's for worse, and nothing can do us part except, of course, death.

I think of Em's beatific smile from this morning, the way her eyes softened as if we were sharing a secret, the secret that would allow us to connect beyond what was happening. A secret between secretly married people.

I've only spent a few days with her and only got a glimpse of the possibility of being with someone like me or, rather, someone who could understand me. Sitting here in this room, this is the only thing I truly miss, her companionship. Not having her here is the biggest source of my distress.

I doze off briefly in a zigzag of non-dreams, colours and electric sand running through my body. I'm aware of where I am and where I'm not.

32

MY FIRST COURT DATE HAPPENS ONE MONTH AFTER MY arrest and bail. My conditions are: no communication with the victim, no weapons, no leaving the city. I don't know what I was expecting, but I was expecting more – having to wear an electronic bracelet on my ankle like a drunk celebrity, getting a camera installed in my bedroom, Net Nanny preventing me from perverting my mind with porn.

Jason comes over every two to three days to torture me with stories about his pathetic dating life. A lot of it happens online. On his desktop, he has folders of links to girls he's approached or is planning to approach: *Yes Girls*, *Maybe Girls* and *No!* (girls who rejected him, but whom he tells himself he didn't want to get with in the first place).

"The crème de la crème," he says, clicking the mouse to close the folders.

"Who fucking says that? *Crème de la crème?*"

He blinks at me. I've offended him. Good.

There's construction being done on my building. New windows being installed. I fantasize about Jason leaving my house and a glass panel falling down from a great height, cutting his head off.

I wave for him to go on. "Don't sulk."

"Okay. Okay. ACAs. I just clean up there. They've got these eyes," Jason's manicured eyebrows form into a worry arch. "Whether they're about to cry or not, they always look like this. You should go. They're really eager to please, it's astonishing. The older ones especially."

"Who?"

"ACAs. Adult Children of Alcoholics. The meetings I go to."

"That's disgusting."

"Is it?" he says. He looks at me, the eyebrows rearranged on his face, one raised.

"Right," I say. I'm the one who's at home awaiting trial for assaulting a young, vulnerable woman.

"Fuck. I miss that bitch so much sometimes," he sighs.

I pat him on the back. The bitch, Candi of the messy tattoos, has gotten back together with her filmmaker boy-friend. They're now making a documentary about the dif-ficult lives of public relations professionals. Jason said they interviewed Gloria.

(On the day of the interview, Gloria was running on three hours of sleep and had a meltdown in front of the camera. The night before, one of her visiting clients, a broken-nosed actor known for playing bad-boy love interests in rom-coms, called her before midnight, high on coke. He wanted to jam and had forgotten his guitar, so Gloria had to locate the owner of a music store that carried his favourite brand of a semi-acoustic. She managed to get the guitar! I can't say I didn't feel impressed and proud when Jason told me about it.)

"Maybe it's a mommy thing for you? With these children of alcoholics?" I say. But I've lost him. He's back to talking about Candi. How she betrayed him, how she had terrible taste in TV shows, how her new boyfriend will have to put up with her poor hygiene – I didn't want to pry but I wanted to ask about *that*; I didn't ask – and how, how, how –

He can't possibly think that this is interesting. He's torturing me because he can. There must be a sense of retribution in being in charge of the person who has always made him feel insecure, to be my surety, to have that power over me.

I never confront him about his reasons for agreeing to bail me out, but I suppose I'm grateful. It really doesn't matter.

In the past few weeks since my arrest, I've resigned myself to various humiliations, big and small. The big ones are losing my job, not being able to leave Canada – where I rarely feel at home anyway; not that I feel at home anywhere, really – having to put the beach house up for sale to pay for my legal fees, putting Dog in the kennel and getting an email from Gloria suggesting that I get in touch with Celia Stone from *Personality* magazine to do an interview "to help your cause!!!"

* * *

The smaller humiliations are Gloria taking Dog from the kennel and fostering him and me agreeing to it because I had no choice and because it was the right thing to do.

Another small humiliation: Writing to Gloria and asking her to forget it after: *would you like to come for a drink?* And Gloria writing back, *Very funny!* This was followed by an invitation to a party celebrating Gloria's engagement to the Polish count.

I buy black curtains on the Internet and same-day courier them to my address. I hang them up. I close the curtains. I disappear. The only time I act human is when Jason comes over. Other than that, who is there to perform for anyway?

I've given up on my workouts. I pace enough.

I've given up cooking. I order food from restaurants that I find online. There's sugar in everything. None of the places are actually what they claim to be: a Korean shows up with food from a Thai place, the pasta sauce on pizza tastes like it comes from a can, the sushi restaurant has Chinese owners. Once, I try an Indian restaurant that actually manages to serve Indian food, but the apartment smells of armpits for days afterwards.

When he comes over to check on me, Jason brings bread and milk and the plainest cereal. Tomatoes, for some reason, but no good cheese. No pâté, no fish. Jason is uninterested in food. He knows how much I enjoy a good meal. I don't say anything about the groceries to him. I won't give him the satisfaction.

* * *

All the time, I think about Em. I know it's not technically *doing* something, but it feels like it, something pleasurable, like going on a little trip. It's my meditation; I can sit still for it. I can rewind the tape in my head a hundred times, analyze every little thing, like the way the light would expose the soft peach fuzz above her lip.

I don't spend too much time on our last encounter, with her sitting on the picnic bench. That's done now, and anyway, there's really not that much of her in it. At least, I don't see how that could possibly be her. She was possessed. A demon with the face of a saint.

At the same time, I understand why she did what she did. I do understand it, on a level where everything makes sense once you add the facts together. The rest is complicated: How do I feel about it?

I rewind the tape of us together, happy, and watch it again. There are hundreds of artifacts to unpack, recall: every inch, every move, every pose, every twitch. I zoom in on her lips, that peach fuzz, things she said. Now a close-up on her breathing, her head on my pillow: my eyes are open in the darkness, watching her.

* * *

My first court appearance occurs somewhere in an alternate universe where people bother with such things.

I sit on a wooden bench. A middle-aged woman with blond hair sits to the left of the judge's bench, transcribing. She looks hefty, German; the hair is sculpted into an old-fashioned wave. Something from the forties, something that Hitler would probably find attractive. I imagine she's wearing a garter belt over a massive pair of panties. See-through hose. *Why can't you be present for once*, says Gloria's voice in my head. *I don't need to be present, Gloria*, I say back in my head.

My lawyer is a fat, sweaty guy named Thomas. He is supposed to be good. He was recommended by my entertainment lawyer. He could've recommended a rubber chicken and I'd have taken him up on it. Thomas has won many cases. *You won't win mine*, I think when he tells me about the many cases he's won.

As we leave the courtroom, I try to catch Hitler's lover's eye, but she's absorbed in her little machine and doesn't look up. I have thirty-five days before the next court date.

33

MY ZEGNA SHOES. MY NEW CHARCOAL VARVATOS SUIT. MY TIE.

No.

No tie.

A McQ T-shirt with an X-ray of a skull on it. Not my style, but I feel murderous. And this is as close as I can get to clubwear. I'm going to a place where all the women try to be Nines – they all have shiny hair and tanned, bouncy breasts. Inside, it will be neon blue or red-and-black, slick. There will be bar stools like stems, and perfect asses sitting on top like flowers. There will be long fingers holding olives on a pick. A curl of yellow garnish swimming in vodka. And fast, brutal club music like a speeding train. Like a train crash.

I open the safe behind my *Keep Calm and Carry On* poster. I pull out a small sandwich bag. I got it when I started dating Gloria. For guests.

No guests now. I don't care for drugs. But it's that kind of night. I'm bored. I want to die. I don't want to die. I'm too bored to die. I want to go out to a bouncy place with bouncy breasts. I pour a tiny amount of the powder onto the surface of my Pedrera coffee table. I wipe the straw with Kleenex, look inside it to make sure it's not clogged. It's not. I break the powder and chop. I'm reminded of cooking.

I separate the powder into five lines. I snort. The bleach hits the back of my throat almost instantly.

I pace around, speeding and rewinding through my *Em* movie.

I snort another line. Pace. Snort. Repeat. Repeat.

I call a taxi. I ask the driver to stop at the first club with a big lineup and a velvet rope. We find one. I get out. I shake hands with the bouncer. He unclicks the rope, twenty dollars richer.

I'm patted up and down by a big, young Indian woman, a Four, looking for drugs or perhaps just wanting to pat me down – it seems her touching goes on a bit too long and there's longing in it, too.

Inside the place, there's a smell. This is an older club. Ghost of cigarette smoke. But fresh shampoo, and the rotting sweetness of alcohol. Cologne mixed with body odours, vanilla-cherry-chocolate Chap Stick. I cut through the crowd, my cocaine body big, smug.

I lock eyes with one of the bartenders. She's got tattooed arms, too much makeup. A heap of black curls above her face. Out of a corner of my eye, I see a blond across the bar smile and look down.

I ask the bartender to send the blond a drink. I ignore the bartender's pissed-off clinking bracelets as she scoops the tip.

* * *

Later on that night, I fuck the bartender in her loft. She rents the place with her *ex*-boyfriend, she says. Ex. The ex-boyfriend is away on a tour with his band. She wants to play me their record after I let it slip about what it is that I do, help records be born, but I pull her onto the bed and flip her over onto her back and start biting the insides of her thighs gently, insistently, like the little fuck-critter that I am. She murmurs something about how the record is shit anyway.

In the morning, she makes me poached eggs. They are barely edible but I'm hungry and hungover, so I eat what's on the plate.

She doesn't touch her food. She sits in the window overlooking a brick wall. She lights a cigarette. She starts talking about her mother, who's a bitch.

"I completely forgot," I say, wiping my mouth. The cigarette smoke makes me nauseous. Or maybe it's the eggs. Either way.

"What?" She looks at me, startled. Without makeup, she looks prettier, younger. I don't tell her this.

I kiss her in the doorway. Her cigarette mouth. She texts me later: *How did it go at the bank?* I don't text her back.

* * *

I go fuck the blond from the bar in her cute uptown townhouse she shares with her boyfriend. The boyfriend is away on a business trip. He had asked her to marry him. She said she needed some time to think about it. She is thinking about it. She says, "I guess this is my last hurrah," to my dick.

"Hurrah," I say, and she giggles.

**

Jenny, Kayla or Kelly, Michelle, Tamika, Julia or July, Kathy with a *K* and Cathy with a *C*, Alicia, Lakshmi, another Jen, Mimi, Some Redhead, a Chinese girl, etcetera. For three weeks, I go from Thursday to Sunday: Varvatos suits, McQ shirts, clubs, clear drinks, pink drinks, amber drinks. Ice cubes. Hot, smooth hands, soft tongues, spit, eyelids, goosebumps, fumbling with the keys, unleashed breasts, legs thrown over my shoulders. Hair spilled all over pillows all over town.

I'm a fucking machine, fucking. Trying to out-fuck what's in my head. My head is full of *her*: her twisting body like a small white wave in the darkness. Her phantom laughter. It cuts through all the noise. It cuts through the yelping and squealing and moaning and whimpering and grunting and slurping. Her *ha ha ha*.

**

"What's wrong?" This one has plump lips, big lips. Her former lovers probably describe them as cock-sucking lips. I can't confirm. My dick refuses to cooperate. I don't care for it to cooperate. I'm exhausted. The dick is exhausted, too full of cocaine. Her breasts try to jump out of a too-small bra. I'm sure she knows that the bra is too small. She wipes her mouth with the back of her hand. She sits back against the wall of pillows. So many pillows propped at the head of her bed. Why does she need so many pillows? Her hair is brown. Unravelling curls that must've taken an hour or more to sculpt. Club-ready hair.

"Are you okay?"

She doesn't ask *Is it me?* the way a plain girl would. A plain girl gone pretty. A Four but a Seven. Someone got to her long before I did. Someone built her up, convinced her she could make all of her confused parts work. Make herself into a whole that would be coherent, attractive. I've nothing to give her. Besides, I don't care to give anyone anything. There's nothing left.

"Not really," I say.

"Does this happen—"

"I'm afraid so," I say.

"Oh, dude, I'm sorry."

"It's okay. It's not you."

"I know that. Shit, that came out totally wrong. You're great. Babe, you're God's gift to women," she squeals. "Just look at you!"

I look at *her*. She smiles like I'm a child who has just shat his pants but it's okay because I'm adorable anyway. I'm God's gift to women

She is the last girl I fuck. Well, try to fuck.

* * *

I spend the last week of my freedom in my apartment.

Jason comes over every day now.

I order groceries online. I cook us elaborate meals. Everything from soufflés to lobster bisque. Beef Wellington.

The last thing I make as a free man is a lemon meringue pie.

I pull the pie out of the oven. Serve it. Then I collapse on my leather sectional, racked by short but powerful, staccato sobs. It's an unexpected outburst. Some dark cellar at my core.

"It must be a comedown from the cocaine," I tell Jason. The fork with sticky meringue is suspended an inch from his open mouth. "A serotonin crash."

"It's just that – I've never seen you cry."

"I'm sorry," I say.

"For what?" he says.

"I'm going to plead guilty."

"I know."

"Good."

"Do you want me to talk you out of it?" he says.

"Absolutely not."

"I wouldn't know how to anyway."

"Good."

34

"HEY," SHE SAYS.

I don't recognize her, and then I do, and I'm not sure which is worse. I hope my face stays neutral; I hope it doesn't show that I don't know how to react. Her hair is full of soft, messy curls, light brown. Her eyebrows are massive and there's dark fuzz above her lip. Hollow cheeks. She was always thin, but this thinness is different; it's unintentional. Too many things are unintentional with her now, except maybe her name.

She no longer calls herself $isi.

"Hey. I like the hair," I say.

"Thanks. It got all curly. Weird." $isi – Sylvia – sits down.

"Thanks for meeting with me. I really appreciate it," I say. "I might be away for some time. A year. Maybe more."

She's not dressed in black; that's different about her too. I can make out the dark shade of her nipples through the white cotton of her blouse. I wonder if it's on purpose. Probably. She hasn't gone entirely granola on me.

"Well. I feel very honoured to be your last date ever. And don't be so dramatic. *I*'ve got at least a few years," she laughs. "But maybe more."

"I'm sorry. I didn't mean –"

"It's okay. Just teasing you. I'm trying not to worry. You know, keeping my hopes up. Being in denial and all that. I was thinking of writing a blog about it, but that's like really admitting it," she says. "Anyway. I'm starting a new treatment in a month. I had to wait for all these tests. I haven't been eating very well. I had fluid building up in my abdomen and I was throwing up a lot, so they thought it was something serious. But it's getting better. I'm getting better."

"You're so young," I say even though I don't mean to say it. Such a cliché. I'm overwhelmed by fear. Not compassion. Fear. It's too unnatural to be so close to dying this early in life. It could happen to anybody, including me.

"What's your point?"

"You shouldn't have to be going through this," I say quickly.

"Aw, thanks. You're such a sweetie pie. I'm feeling better than I have in a really long time. So I'm ready to get back to active treatment."

"And then?"

"And then we'll see. I didn't think it would come back. But you learn how to deal with things. I suppose the only difference between me and everyone else is that I have a vague idea of when I *might* be kicking the bucket. But, you know, those things are."

"I know many people who –"

"Yes. I know. Everyone knows many people," she says. "Do you, really?"

"No. I don't. I just don't know what to say."

"It's not about you. Don't worry about it. It's nice to see you," she says. "And I know that you didn't do it. That's why I'm here, right? To absolve you of your sins!"

I feel myself blush. I phoned her deep into the night a few nights ago. I'm not close with anyone. There's Jason, but there's only so much *bro* I can take. I needed a girl, and not Gloria. Someone less bitter, someone younger, more open. And $isi and I have history. Sylvia.

I phoned and asked her if I was possibly losing my mind, if maybe I actually was the violent guy that Em said I was. A guy who could hurt women. I was not that guy. But I got myself into a state where I started to doubt reality. Sylvia didn't hang up. "You're a fucking jerk. But yeah, you're not that kind of guy," she said.

"I wanted to find out how you were doing too," I say, now.

"I'm doing better. I'm doing really well," she sighs.

A waitress shows up to take our orders. She has a pretty face, big, trusting eyes that make you imagine her sliding down your stomach, looking up at you. A freckled nose. No waist and small breasts, but a nice butt. A Four.

Sylvia says, "That's the worst thing about it. Knowing when you might die."

"You're not going to die."

"Sure I am. You are too. But you're better off not knowing."

I think how absurd it is for her to suggest that I'm going to die, but it's more absurd of me to think that that's absurd.

The waitress comes back with our food. A salad for Sylvia and a burger for me. The fries are too greasy, and the bun is dry. The pickle looks exhausted. I think about ordering a beer but decide against it. The waitress looks at me for a moment too long.

"It looks delicious," I say. I smile at the waitress with my eyes.

"Thank you," Sylvia says.

The waitress walks away. She's got a nice walk, a nice swaying bounce in her hips.

Sylvia says, "I think it's strange when girls don't have waists, don't you?" Her cattiness could be because the waitress doesn't recognize her, but most likely it's jealousy.

Our meeting isn't too long. For a while, Sylvia talks about her mother, whom she's become close with. Her mother quit smoking. They are going to Cuba together in the winter.

"It's hard to get good vegetables in Cuba." I'm proud of myself for remembering the weird diet that she's on. Ten cups of vegetables a day. They wrote about it on some gossip website.

"Communists don't believe in vegetables?" she says.

"What kind of vegetables do you have to eat?"

"Squash, broccoli, peas, carrots, asparagus," she says and pulls out her phone to check the rest. I look down at my plate, at my untouched burger.

"I should send you some recipes. There's a very easy butternut squash pasta dish—"

"Raw vegetables, Guy. I can't boil them." She smiles at me like I'm annoying.

The waitress asks if we want any desserts but we don't. I ask for the bill.

Sylvia talks some more. There's a boyfriend, a guy she met in Alcoholics Anonymous who is "really talented."

The waitress hands me the bill. The waitress's name is Amy. I think about writing my phone number on the bill but decide against it.

I have an acute understanding of what *feeling empty* means. I feel vastly, tragically empty, like there was no past and there is no future.

35

FOR MY SENTENCING, I DRESS IN A SUIT. I BUY IT ESPECIALLY
for this occasion. It might seem stupid to buy yourself a suit
right before you go to jail, yet this is precisely why I get it. I
need to reassure myself that this, going to jail, is in no way
the end of my life. I pay extra to have the suit altered on
the same day.

I wait for my suit in a cheerfully clean, cream-coloured
coffee place in a shopping district. It seems surreal that right
now I am here and tomorrow I will be incarcerated. I drink
my tiny cappuccino, my pinky raised.

I watch the fat tourists going in and out of high-end shops.
Small packages. They can only afford wallets, scarves, belts.
But they seem happy. When they come out, their eyes are
feverish. Fuck it, they've got credit cards. They can always
take on some extra shifts! You only live once! In contrast,
the expensively bored cuntpets of rich men – women who
can afford everything – look miserable. Massive parcels. The
bigger the unhappiness, the bigger the parcels.

I watch the older ones with stretched, pinched faces – veterans of diets and loneliness. The younger ones trot on legs like needles, expertly not tripping over their fluffy white dogs, one bony hand clutching plastic bags packed with tiny doggie turds, the other hand wrapped around enormous cups full of zero-calorie froth. Many of these women are too skinny to fuck. I cannot imagine myself fucking them.

I order another coffee. There's a new girl behind the counter. She's got dark skin, a big ass.

"Oh my god, you look like that actor," she says.

"My wife said the same thing. That's how we met."

She shows her bottom teeth. "Cool."

I try to jerk off twice in the toilet. I imagine the coffee girl sitting on my face. The sweet, musky smell of her. My tongue in her ass. Her disgusted face as I try to kiss her afterwards. I'm half-erect. I can't get myself inspired.

Later on, I try on my new Paul Smith wool suit. The colour is called *anthracite*, which is coal, which means black. It's a black suit; the suit is black. The sales clerk claps his hands. I'm not irritated by this. I want to clap as well. I look great. I take a picture in the mirror and send it to Henri, my old shopping consultant. He sends back a picture of himself giving a thumbs-up.

I wish I could send a picture to Em. *Look, Em. Your man. Such a beautiful man with perfect skin. What a nice body. All of it contoured into this fine suit. A perfect male form, perfectly useless now. Look. All for you.*

36

WHEN WE'RE NOT WORKING WE CAN WATCH TV. WE GET CABLE here. We watch the news. One inmate's wife was gunned down on the outside. He first found out about it on the news.

We get newspapers. There are computers although there is no Internet. We get board games. The board games are almost as popular as getting high in here.

You can ask for sketchbooks and crayons. It's good for us. Each request is assessed on its own merits and according to a list of approved items. There are carefully monitored cell inventories. My cell is always impeccable. I don't abuse my privileges. I don't get high. I behave when I'm in the shop. I blank, emboss and finish licence plates. I behave during roll call, in the kitchen, cleaning cells, working out at the gym.

I don't pace here. I'm good at being locked down. If I get anxious, I do sit-ups and push-ups. When I'm not anxious, I read or watch TV. This is how I come across the Tarantino film *Kill Bill*. I've never seen it. It was quite a big deal back when it first came out. I wish I had seen it.

It's a violent movie. I don't know why we're allowed to watch it. Maybe because it's *funny*-violent. Heads flying off, swords slicing off arms, ha ha ha. A slapstick of splattering blood. I don't care for that stuff. Yet I'm drawn to it because of the lead, played by Uma Thurman. The lead is a sweat-soaked, nostril-pumping character named Bride. She kills her former colleagues and her former boss and lover, Bill (played by David Carradine), who tried to kill her in the past.

Before Bill dies, they forgive each other. I laugh out loud when I figure it out. *Bride.* The granny rapist next to me shouts to "shut the fuck up" and I shut the fuck up because I suddenly don't feel like laughing at all.

* * *

"She was so beautiful in it, wasn't she?" Em says. "I watched that movie after a difficult breakup and it really helped."

"You said you've never been in love."

"That's right. I wasn't in love. I was just annoyed at having been dumped. That's all." She shifts in her chair. Yawns. Raises her arms quickly to stretch, shakes her head at the guard who starts walking up to us. "Everything okay?"

The guard likes her, I can tell. The guard looks like one of those guys in PUA basements. I can tell he's having trouble getting women. I can picture him sweating discreetly, trying to impress her, listing his accomplishments. He enjoys going to the movies. He peaked in high school.

"Everything's okay," she says softly.

(When I first sat down, I watched her closely. I assumed this was her first time in a prison visiting room. I didn't want her to be uncomfortable. I had words of support ready: *Just pretend this is a movie*. But her face was all indifference behind black-framed glasses. What kind of person isn't anxious about visiting prison for the first time? At the other end of the room, an inmate lunged at the woman sitting opposite him. The guards shouted, swarmed the table. He didn't fight the guards. They walked him out of the room. Em took off her glasses and wiped the lenses with her sleeve.)

"Everything's okay," I say.

The guard walks away. His body stiffens. He tries to make himself look bigger. She's not looking at him. She drums on the table with her fingers. Her hard nails are shiny and red. The red matches her outfit. She gives me a quick, forced smile.

I smile back. "You look great."

"Oh yeah?" she says.

Her hair is dyed dark blond; it's shoulder-length. It's hair used to being outside in the sun. Possibly used to having fingers woven through it. I try very hard not to ask. Is someone doing that? Waving his sausage fingers through her hair?

She's heavier now. The pounds sit on her bones, weighing her down, making her seem hunched. She's too skinny to handle being this fat.

She's wearing a bright red dress. She must be wearing it to divert attention from her tired face. The colour does exactly the opposite, making her seem older. It's an unusual colour to wear in here. Most visitors try to be anonymous. The two of us must look like some weird Halloween decoration. An orange squash and a tomato in the bland, white room.

"You don't get the Internet here? It was all over the celeb sites. Your girl has retired," she says.

"Who?"

"$isi. She has a blog now. It's all about cancer. But it's all good news, don't freak out. Her treatment is working. But she's done with music. Too bad."

"Too bad," I say, but I feel immense relief. Almost euphoric relief. As if I'd been forgiven.

"You really okay?" she says after we don't talk for a while. This is fine, not talking. It's more than doing something romantic like sitting and holding hands together and talking. If you can be silent together, that's a good sign.

"I'm really okay. You?"

"Okay too. Really. Busy. Finished making my first audio for a movie. It was stressful. I shouldn't complain."

"What's the film about?"

"Nothing you'd find especially sexy. But it's about music, so it's a bit up your alley. I'll try to remember to mail it to you when it's done."

"I'm proud of you."

"Mmmhmm."

"I really am."

"You don't need to be proud of me. I've got people to be proud of me," she says a bit too loudly. "Sorry. God. That's not what I meant."

"It is. And it's okay. You're throwing a tantrum. But you're right. You probably have lots of people to be proud of you. So I'm just going to be proud independently if that's okay."

She sighs. "Yeah."

"Why are you here?" I say, even though I'm afraid. What's the worst answer she could give? She's curious. That's the worst answer. Nothing else. Or she's cruel. That's a bad answer, too. Pulling wings off a fly.

She says nothing for a while. "Why did you plead guilty?"

"Why?"

The guard is watching us again. Or watching her. To him, the red dress probably signals all kinds of things. She wants *it*. She wants *him*. Only sluts wear red.

I was guilty. Not of raping her, but of betraying myself. I'm not here because of my nature, like the pedophile in the cell across from me, or the granny rapist. I'm here because I went against my nature. I am also here because I liked going against my nature.

I called Gloria from here once. She was hysterical. I should appeal. Could she contact Thomas the lawyer? She'd never stopped loving me! I couldn't calm her down. "Why are you so fucked up? What are you, some kind of masochist? You're not a masochist! You only think of yourself," she shouted.

She was confused. I had to hang up.

* * *

I think of my dream from long ago, running through the forest. My face smeared with blood, my feet turned into hairy paws sinking into mossy ground. I was hunting. No. I was being hunted. Em catching up with me and sinking her teeth into my artery. *Gotcha*.

I could free myself. Protest my innocence like a stupid little bitch. Call in favours: Gloria, the Grey Campaign people, $isi. Character witnesses. Petitions. My passion for good causes. My selflessness. My martyrdom. We could find holes in Em's setup. Proof it was consensual. No tears in vaginal walls, no bruises on the insides of her thighs.

I want to say things to her. *It was all for you.*

"Fifteen minutes!" the guard yells.

"How is Dolores?" I say

Em sits up straight, her shoulders pushing back. There's a slight twitch in the corner of her mouth. "We're not friends anymore. But she's okay. I think."

"You're not friends."

"She dropped out of school after she met you, after the accident, and went to a loony bin for a bit and came back and got engaged and married some loser. She never left our hometown. The end. I was so mad at her. I blamed you, but I was also mad at her, if you need to know."

"Has she said anything about—"

"Nope. She just moved on. We never really talked. She met her idiot husband in the psych ward. I went to her wedding and the baby shower. And then we lost touch. That's all."

I wish I could slide right next to her. She sits with her elbows on the table. Oh, to touch those elbows. Feel their hardness. Take her head in my hands. Force her to look at me.

"Was she in on it?"

Em shakes her head. "God, no."

Sometimes I imagined both of them plotting. The two of them sitting on their girly beds. $isi blasting on the speakers. Newspaper clippings about me strewn around. Lots of giggling. A pile of limbs and hugs. Dolores. Open mouth. Protesting. Em outlining a particularly brutal detail (the choking). Or, conversely, Dolores egging Em on. Dolores coming up with the particularly brutal detail.

I'm relieved it was just Em. Her own crazy idea. That's how much it mattered. *I* mattered. We are in this together. I feel bonded to her. Married. Another freedom that I would give up for her if she'd let me.

She will let me. Her visit to me is a weakness. She has this weakness and I am it. This is the opening in her, to her. I wish I could reach across this table, feel the warmth of her blood pulsing underneath the pale skin. I would grab the back of her neck. I would smash her chapped lips against mine.

I finally say it.

She looks at me and says nothing. We both look around the room, stopping once in a while to take a break in each other's eyes. I hold her this way. She lets me hold her. We could be talking right now, but what's the point? We are saying everything we need to say.

Before she leaves, she leans forward – that guard watching us, inching closer. She says, "Wait for you."

"Wait for me." Is there or isn't there a man weaving his fingers through her hair? It doesn't matter. The tiredness that seems to permanently reside in her ashen skin signals trouble. I will never make her look this way.

I reach out to grab her hands. The guard starts walking toward us. "Hands," he shouts. She starts to pull her hands out of my grip. *No. Please.*

She stops struggling.

We'll go through years of sexual discovery. Years of sexual plateaus. Years of headaches, lies, infidelities. Reconciliations and – what else? – apathy. It's better than nothing. I have nothing. This is me capitulating to love. I am its ultimate conquest. I've always wanted to cheat it, give it as if it was mine to give. I've never meant a word of it. And here I am with a fluttering chest. Inside me, this love like a heart attack. Imprisoning me for life. Because this is for life, this will be a life sentence, her loving me.

Wait for me.

"I said *hands*," the guard barks right in my ear.

Hands. I let go of her hands. The past is no longer important; the future is a possibility. I cannot feel the emptiness anymore – I cannot feel what isn't there. She smiles. This is the first real smile she's given me today. Maybe the first real smile she's given anyone in a long time. It seems to shatter a thin veneer of sadness that's accumulated on her face. I can see all of her hidden beauty, its secret kept from the needy, predatory world.

The End

THANK YOU:

*The crew at Wolsak & Wynn Publishers
and Buckrider Books:*
Paul Vermeersh
Noelle Allen
Emily Dockrill Jones
Ashley Hisson
Joe Stacey

Designer Michel Vrana
My literary agent, Chris Bucci

Friends and family:
Stacey Madden
Danila Botha
Neil Sharma
Laura Bydlowska
Russell Smith
Erin Kobayashi
Tim Rostron
Sheila Heti
Joseph Boyden

The Ontario Arts Council
and the Canada Council for the Arts

Jowita Bydlowska was born in Warsaw, Poland, and moved to Canada as a teen. She is the author of the bestselling memoir *Drunk Mom*. A journalist and fiction writer, she lives in Toronto, Canada.